ROAD TRIP WITH THE ELIGIBLE BACHELOR

ROAD TRIP WITH THE ELIGIBLE BACHELOR

MICHELLE DOUGLAS

MILLS & BOON

First published in Great Britain 2018
by Mills & Boon, an imprint of HarperCollins*Publishers*
1 London Bridge Street, London, SE1 9GF

Large Print edition 2019

© 2018 Michelle Douglas

ISBN: 978-0-263-07891-6

MIX
Paper from
responsible sources
FSC C007454

This book is produced from independently certified
FSC™ paper to ensure responsible forest management.
For more information visit www.harpercollins.co.uk/green.

Printed and bound in Great Britain
by CPI Group (UK) Ltd, Croydon, CR0 4YY

To my gorgeous nephew, Josh—
hero and all-round good guy.

CHAPTER ONE

'HELLO.' QUINN LAVERTY tried to find a smile for the customer service clerk on the other side of the counter. She raised her voice to be heard above the jostling crowd. 'I'm here to collect the car I booked.'

'Name, please?'

Quinn gave him her details and tried to slide her credit card free from its slot in her purse with one hand. Chase hung off her other hand, all of his six-year-old weight balanced on one leg and her arm as he stretched as far as he could reach along the counter with his toy car, making the requisite 'broom-broom' noises.

She made him straighten and stand on two legs and then grimaced at the customer beside her who'd been 'driven over' by said toy car. 'I'm sorry.'

'No problem at all.'

He flashed her a smile and she found herself smiling back. Nice smile. *Really* nice eyes. Actually...

She frowned. There was something faintly familiar about him. She stared and then shook herself and shrugged it off, turning back to the clerk. It might just be that he was the exact model of son her father had always wanted—clean-cut, professional and respectable. She did her best not to hold that against him.

Speaking of sons...

She glanced to her left. Robbie leaned with his back against the counter and stared up at the ceiling, his face dreamy. Quinn tried to channel some of his calm. She hadn't expected this all to take so long.

Mind you, when she'd booked the car over a month ago she hadn't thought there'd be a national plane strike either.

'I'm afraid there's been a slight change to the model of car you booked.'

Her attention spun back to the clerk. 'What kind of change?'

'Ow!' Chase pulled his hand from hers and glared.

'Sorry, honey.' She smoothed down his hair and smiled at him, but a fist tightened in her chest. She glanced back at the clerk. 'What kind of change?' she repeated.

'We no longer have that model of car available.'

But she'd booked it a whole month ago especially!

The commotion in the car rental office didn't die down. Beside her she sensed her neighbour's frustration growing too. *'I have to leave Perth today!'* He didn't shout, but every word was clipped and strong.

He glanced at her and she suddenly realised she was staring. She sent him a buck-up smile and turned back to the clerk, doing her best to block out all the background noise. 'I'm driving across the Nullarbor Plain. I need a car that can go the distance.'

'I understand the reasons you booked a four-wheel drive, Mrs Laverty, but we just don't have any available.'

Brilliant.

She didn't bother correcting him on the *Mrs*. People made that assumption all the time.

She lifted her chin, preparing for a fight. 'I have a lot of luggage to fit into the car.' Another reason she'd chosen a four-wheel drive.

'Which is why we've upgraded you.'

Was that what they called it? She folded her arms. She'd chosen the car she had because of its safety and reliability rating. As far as fuel efficiency went it was one of the best too. It was the perfect car to take them across the country.

'We've upgraded you to a late model station wagon.'

'Does it have four-wheel drive?'

'No, ma'am.'

Quinn closed her eyes briefly, but all that did was underscore the scent of desperation and outrage in the air.

'I want to speak to the manager,' the man beside her clipped out.

'But, sir—'

'Now!'

She drew in a breath and opened her eyes. 'I need a four-wheel drive. The fuel consumption on that wagon will be outrageous and as I'll be travelling to New South Wales in it that's an awful lot of fuel.' She'd be driving the car for forty hours. Probably more. 'And, I might add, with none of the benefits the four-wheel drive offers.'

Driving suddenly seemed like the stupidest idea a woman had ever had. She lifted her chin another notch. 'Thank you, but I don't want an upgrade. I want the car I originally booked.'

The clerk scratched his nose and shuffled his feet, staring everywhere but at her. 'The thing is, ma'am, with the plane strike, you understand there just aren't any four-wheel drives currently available.'

'But I booked this over a month ago!'

'I understand and I do apologise. We won't be charging you for the upgrade. In fact, we'll be offering you a discount and a credit voucher.'

That was something at least. Quinn couldn't afford to stray too far from the budget she'd set herself.

'And the crux of the matter is...' the clerk leaned confidentially across the counter '...there isn't anything else available.' He gestured to the crowded room behind Quinn. 'If you don't want the station wagon we'll have plenty of other takers who will.'

She glanced back behind her too and grimaced.

'I can't guarantee when a four-wheel drive vehicle will become available.'

She bit back a sigh. 'We'll take it.' She didn't have any other option. They'd sold up practically everything they owned. The lease on their house had run out and new tenants were expected within the next few days. Their lives no longer belonged here in Perth. Besides, she'd made a booking at a caravan park in Merredin for this afternoon. She didn't want to lose her booking fee on that as well.

'Excellent. I just need you to sign here and here.'

Quinn signed and then followed the clerk out through a side door. She made sure both boys had their backpacks—they'd refused to leave them with the rest of the luggage back at the house.

'Keep the paperwork on you. You'll need it for the Newcastle office. And if you'll just wait here the car will be brought around in a jiffy.'

'Thank you.'

The relative quiet out here after the cacophony in the office was bliss.

Robbie sat on a nearby bench and swung his feet. Chase immediately knelt on the ground beside the bench and 'broom-broomed' his toy car around.

'I'm sorry, Mr Fairhall, I wish I could help you. I have your card so if something comes up I'll let you know immediately.'

Fairhall? That was it! She'd known she'd seen

him before. She turned to confirm it anyway. Uh huh, her neighbour at the service counter had been none other than Aidan Fairhall, up-and-coming politician. He'd been travelling the country canvassing for support. He had hers.

He had a nice on-air manner too. No doubt it was all orchestrated as these things were, but he came across as intelligent and polite.

Polite shouldn't be overrated. In her opinion there should be more of it. Especially in politics.

She watched him slump onto a neighbouring bench as the man with the manager badge pinned to his shirt strode away. His shoulders drooped and he dropped his head to his hands. He raked his hands through his hair and then suddenly froze. He glanced up at her—a long sidelong look from beneath his hand—and she swallowed, re-alising she'd been caught out staring at him *twice* now.

He straightened. Her heart did a crazy little thump-thump. She swallowed and shrugged. 'I couldn't help overhearing. I'm sorry.'

He smiled, but she sensed the strain behind it. 'It looks as if you've had more luck.'

Her lips twisted. 'Considering I booked this car over a month ago...'

He let out a breath, nodded. 'It'd be very poor form if they cancelled it on you at this late date.'

'But they're not giving us the car we wanted,' Robbie piped up.

She should've known he'd been listening. His dreamy expression lulled her every single time. 'But it's a better one,' she said, because she didn't want him to worry. Robbie had taken to worrying about everything.

'We're moving house,' Chase declared, glancing up from his car. 'All the way across the world!'

'Country,' she corrected.

Chase stared at her and then nodded. 'Country,' he repeated. 'Can we move to the moon?'

'Not this week.' She grinned. Robbie and Chase—her darling boys—they made it all worthwhile.

'It sounds exciting,' Mr Fairhall said. He glanced at Robbie. 'And if you're in an even better car now that probably means your trip is going to be lucky too.'

She liked him then. Amid his own troubles he found the time to be nice to a couple of young boys—and not just nice but reassuring. If he hadn't already won her vote he'd have had it now.

'The plane strike seems to be turning the country on its head. I hope it ends soon so you can be where you need to be.'

He must have a crazy schedule. Actually—she rested one hand on a hip and surveyed him—maybe this would prove a blessing in disguise. He looked tired. A rest from the hurly-burly might do him the world of good.

His eyes darkened with some burden that would have to remain nameless because she had no intention of asking about it. 'Rumour has it that things on that front are going to take…' his shoulders sagged '…time.'

She winced.

'Mrs Laverty?' A man bounced out from behind the wheel of a white station wagon. 'Your car.'

She nodded as he handed her the keys with a cheery, 'Safe driving.'

'Thank you.'

Mr Fairhall rose. 'You boys have a great journey, okay?' And as he spoke he lifted their backpacks into the back of the wagon.

'Can I sit back here with the backpacks?' Chase asked, climbing in beside them.

'Most certainly not,' she countered, lifting him

out again. 'Thank you,' she said to Mr Fairhall as he closed the wagon.

'Where are you going when the planes work again?' Chase asked as Quinn ushered him around to the back seat.

'Sydney.'

'That's near where we're going,' Robbie said. 'We looked it up on the map.' He pulled out the map he'd been keeping in his shorts pocket.

The swift glance her polite politician sent her then had her stomach tightening.

'You're going to Sydney?'

She shifted her weight from one foot to the other. 'A couple of hours north of Sydney.'

'You wouldn't consider...?'

He broke off, no doubt in response to the rictus of a smile that had frozen to her face.

'No, of course not,' he said softly, as if to himself.

The boys glanced from her to him and back again.

Darn it! This was supposed to be a *family* trip. This road trip was about giving the boys a holiday...with the opportunity to ask her whatever questions they wanted about this new life they were embarking upon. In a relaxed atmosphere.

Another person—a stranger—would throw those dynamics out completely.

She made herself brisk. 'C'mon, boys, in the car. Seat belts fastened, please.'

Aidan Fairhall nodded at her. 'Safe trip.'

'Thank you.'

Darn it. Darn it. Darn it.

He moved back to the bench. She stowed her handbag, made sure the kids had their seat belts fastened and then moved to the driver's seat. She glanced at Mr Fairhall and bit her lip.

'He wanted to come with us,' Chase said.

Why did children have to be so perceptive when you didn't want them to be and so obtuse when you did?

'You always tell us we should help people when they need it,' Robbie pointed out.

She turned in her seat and surveyed them both. 'You'd like to invite Mr Fairhall along on our journey?'

Robbie stared back. 'How'd you know his name?'

'I've seen him on the television. He's a politician.'

'Would he come all the way with us?'

'I'm not sure. As soon as the plane strike ends he might jump ship at any place that has an airport.'

'He's a nice man,' Chase said.

She had a feeling Chase was right.

Robbie studied the object of their conjecture and then turned back. 'He looks kinda sad.'

'Yeah.' She tried not to let those slumped shoulders pluck too hard at her. It was just… She knew exactly how that felt—the defeat, the worry and the helplessness.

'It might make our trip luckier,' Robbie said.

She couldn't mistake the hope in his eyes. She bit her lip to stop from saying something rash. Her eldest son ached for a male role model and the knowledge cut at her. Not that she expected Aidan Fairhall to fill that role. Still…

She blew out a breath and wound down the passenger side window. 'Mr Fairhall?'

He glanced up.

'We've just had a family conference.'

He stood. He wasn't terribly tall—he might be six feet—but he had a lean athletic body that moved with effortless grace. She watched him approach—stared as he approached—and her mouth started to dry and her heart started to pound. She tried to shake herself out from under the spell, only she found she'd frozen in position. She wished now she hadn't called him over. With a superhuman effort she cleared her throat. 'As we're…uh…all headed in the same direction we thought if you would like a lift all or part of the way…'

He blinked. Hope lit his face, making it truly beautiful, firing his brown eyes with a light that made her swallow. They weren't a boring brown, but a deep amber that brought to mind blazing hearth fires, fine brandies and rich caramel.

Then the light in those beautiful eyes faded and for some reason her heart sank too. Maybe it was the unspoken judgement she recognised in those deep amber depths. She sat back a little. She swallowed. 'I'm not given to recklessness, Mr Fairhall. I recognised you and I like your public persona. I like your education policies more.'

His lips twisted but the darkness faded from his eyes. His fingers drummed against the roof of the car.

'But, as I don't actually know you, and if you do take us up on our very kind offer, I'll be informing the manager of this car hire company that you'll be accompanying us. I'll also be ringing my aunt to tell her the same.' He didn't say anything. She shrugged and forced herself to add, 'But if we can help you out in any way then we'd be happy to.'

'Why would you do that?'

'People should help each other out always,' her earnest eldest son said.

'And you looked sad,' Chase added.

The light in those amazing eyes faded again, although the lips kept their smile.

Quinn rushed on. 'Also, it'd be nice to share some of the driving...not to mention the fuel costs. I'm afraid it wouldn't precisely be a free ride.' She'd sensed that would go against the grain with him.

There was a long silence. Quinn kicked herself. 'I'm sorry we have you at a disadvantage. I'm Quinn Laverty and these are my sons, Robbie and Chase.' She fished her licence out and handed it to him as proof of both her identity and the fact she could drive. 'If you decide to accompany us I'd want you to phone someone to let them know about your plans and who you're travelling with.'

He handed the licence back to her. 'I'm not given to recklessness either, Mrs Laverty.'

She didn't bother correcting the *Mrs*. 'Quinn,'

she said instead. As she had no intention of becoming romantically involved with any man, let alone a politician—dear God!—the *Mrs* provided her with another level of protection.

Not that she needed protection from unwanted suitors. She could squash them flat as easily as swatting bugs. But correcting that Mrs might give the wrong impression.

Aidan Fairhall was from her parents' world and she had no intention of returning to that world. *Ever.*

She shuddered. Another long silence ensued. Eventually she cleared her throat. 'I'm sorry to hurry you, Mr Fairhall, but we'd really like to get going soon.'

Aidan's gaze snapped to Quinn Laverty's. 'If it was just work commitments I wouldn't dream of imposing on you like this.' His father would hit the roof if he ever heard Aidan utter that sentiment. 'But...' He hesitated.

'But?'

She had an unhurried way of speaking that was restful.

'I have a family commitment I have to meet.'

'Like I said, if we can help...'

She'd probably harangue him the entire way, pointing out all the flaws in his proposed policies, but… He had a sudden vision of his mother's worn eyes. He nodded. The alternative was worse. He made his lips curve upwards even though the heaviness in his heart made that nearly impossible. 'I will be forever in your debt. Thank you, I'd very much like to take you up on your very kind offer.' He pulled his cell phone from his pocket and gestured the manager back over.

Quinn spoke to the manager.

Aidan rang his mother.

As he expected, she fretted at the news. 'But you don't even know this woman, darling, and it's such a long way to drive. How do you know you'll be safe?'

He tried to allay her fears. Not very successfully. Eventually he said, 'If it will make you happier, I'll remain in Perth until the plane strike is over.' He had to grit his teeth as he said it. He had to remind himself there were a lot of reasons for her anxieties and apprehensions.

'But you must be back in time for the party!'

Yes. He bit back a sigh. He must be back in time for the party. Still, it was a fortnight away.

'Harvey thinks the industrial action will be protracted. He's talking seven whole days. I can't get a train or bus ticket out of the place or hire a car for the next week. Everything is booked solid.'

'Oh, dear.'

He didn't need to see her to know the way her hands fluttered about her throat. 'This is my best option. As soon as the strike ends, I'll make my way to the nearest airport and be home as soon as I can.'

'Oh, dear.'

'I really don't think there's anything to worry about, Mother.' And movement of any kind beat kicking his heels in Perth.

There was a slight pause. 'Of course you must do what you think best, darling.'

And thereby she absolved herself of any responsibility and placed it all squarely on Aidan's shoulders. He tried not to bow under its weight. 'I'll call you this evening.'

He collected his overnight case and stowed it in the back. 'You travel light,' Quinn observed.

He slid into the passenger seat. 'I was only supposed to be in Perth for a single night.'

She started the car up and eased it out of the car park and onto the road. 'It's a long way to come for just a day.'

'Two days,' he corrected. 'And one night.'

He thought she might glance at him then, but she kept her eyes on the road. 'I see you're a man who knows how to make the most of his time.'

'That's me.'

Quinn Laverty had a blonde ponytail and wore a kind of crazy oversized tie-dyed dress that covered her to her ankles. She wasn't exactly a flower power child, but there was something of the hippy about her.

The longer he stared at her, the more he wanted to keep staring. Crazy. He loosened his tie a fraction and turned to the boys. 'Robbie and Chase, it's great to meet you. Thank you for letting me share your journey.'

'You're welcome, Mr Fairhall,' the elder, Robbie, said with perfect manners.

He could see the path set out for the boy now— school prefect, school captain, dux, university medal and then a high-powered job in the public service.

What a nightmare!

Only for you.

He pushed the thought away. 'If it's okay with your mother you can call me Aidan.'

Quinn glanced at him briefly. Her lips tilted up into an easy smile. 'That's okay with me.'

Ten minutes later they stopped at an unprepossessing house and loaded the back of the car with an assortment of boxes and suitcases. The backpacks moved onto the back seat with the boys. Aidan insisted on doing all the heavy lifting.

'See you, Perth,' Quinn said with a jaunty wave at the house.

Both boys waved too.

'Can we play our Gameboys now?' Chase asked.

'You can.'

Both boys whooped and dived into their backpacks. She glanced at Aidan and rolled her eyes. 'They were specially bought for the trip.'

Probably quite a financial outlay for a single mum. Not that he had any proof that she was single.

'And the deal was that they weren't allowed to play them until the trip itself started.'

Smart move. Those things would keep the boys occupied for hours, which, quite obviously, had been her plan. He settled back in his seat as the suburbs of Perth passed by one after the other. 'I know the clerk back at the store called you Mrs Laverty, but I also notice you're not wearing a wedding ring.' He kept his tone neutral. He didn't want her thinking he was judging her or condemning her in any way. 'Are you married or single or...'

Her brows lifted. 'Does it matter?'

He loosened his tie a tiny bit more. 'Not at all. But some people get fixated on titles so I always like to get them straight.'

'I prefer Ms.'

Which told him precisely nothing at all. When he met her gaze, she laughed. Sparkling green eyes momentarily dazzled him. 'You first,' she dared.

A question like that would normally have him sitting up straighter. Instead he found himself chuckling and relaxing back into his seat even more. 'Single. Most definitely single. Never been married; hence, never been divorced and not currently in a relationship.'

'Ditto,' she said.

'So, are you moving back home? Is Newcastle where you grew up?'

'No.'

Her face shuttered closed—not completely but in a half-fan—and he bit back a sigh. False start number one.

A moment's silence ensued and then she turned to him with a smile that was too bright. 'Is your campaign going well?'

He bit back a curse. Was that all people could think to converse with him about—his darn job? 'Yes.'

Another moment's silence. False start number two. For pity's sake, he was good at small talk. He opened his mouth. He closed it again. The deep heaviness in his chest grew. Normally he could push it away, ignore it, but today it gave him no quarter. It was this stupid plane strike and the break in his routine. It had given him time to think.

Thinking wouldn't help anything!

She glanced at him, her face sober, and he knew then that she was going to bring up the subject he most dreaded. He wanted to beg her not to, but years of *good* breeding prevented him.

'How are you and your parents now, since your brother...?'

That was a different approach to most, but... The heaviness started to burn and ache. He rested his head back against his seat and tried to stop his lip from curling.

'I'm sorry. Don't answer that. It was a stupid

thing to ask. Grieving in public must be harrowing. I just wanted to say I'm truly sorry for your loss, Aidan.'

The simple words with their innate sincerity touched him and the burn in his chest eased a fraction. 'Thank you, Quinn.'

Two beats passed. Quinn shuffled in her seat a little and her ponytail bounced. 'I'm moving to an olive farm.'

He straightened and turned to her. 'An olive farm?'

'Uh-huh.' She kept her eyes on the road, but she was grinning. 'I bet that's not a sentence you hear every day, is it?'

'It's not a sentence I have ever heard uttered in my life.'

'It's probably not as startling as saying I was moving to an alpaca farm or going to work on a ferret breeding programme. But it's only a degree or two behind.'

She'd made things good—or, at least, better—just like that. With one abrupt and startling admission. 'What do you know about olives?'

She lifted her nose in the air. 'I know that marinated olives on a cheese platter is one of life's little pleasures.'

He laughed. She glanced at him and her eyes danced. 'What about you; what do you know about olives?'

'That they grow on trees. That they make olive oil. And that marinated olives on a cheese platter is one of life's little pleasures.'

She laughed then too and he couldn't remember a sound he'd ever enjoyed more. He closed his eyes all the better to savour it. It was the last thing he remembered.

Aidan sat bolt upright and glanced around. He was alone in the car. He peered at his watch.

He closed his eyes and shook his right arm, but when he opened them again the time hadn't changed. He'd slept for two hours?

He pressed his palms to his eyes and dragged in a breath before stretching to the right and then the left to ease the cricks in his back and neck. Finally he took stock of his surroundings. Quinn had parked beneath a huge old gum tree to give him shade. At the moment she, Robbie and Chase kicked a ball around on a big oval in front of him. She'd hitched her dress up to mid-thigh into a pair of bike shorts.

His eyes widened. Man, she was…fit!

He shook his head and pressed fingers to his eyes again.

With bones that literally creaked, he pushed out of the car and stretched. Warm air caressed his skin and he slid his suit jacket off to lay it on the front seat. Quinn waved and then pointed behind him to an amenities block. 'They're clean and well maintained,' she called out.

He lifted a hand to let her know he'd heard.

When he returned he found her sitting cross-legged on a blanket at the edge of the oval beside an assortment of bags.

'Where are we?'

'Wundowie.'

He pulled out his smart phone and searched for it on the Internet. 'We've been travelling…'

'Nearly two and a half hours, though we're still only about an hour out of Perth. There was a lot of traffic,' she said in answer to his raised eyebrow. 'And there was some mini-marathon we had to be diverted around.' She shrugged. 'It all took time. Would you like a sandwich or an apple?' She opened a cooler bag and proffered its contents towards him. 'Or water? There's plenty here.'

He reached for a bottle of water. 'Thank you, I'm parched.'

'But well rested,' she said with a laugh.

His hand clenched about the water bottle, making the plastic crackle. 'You should've woken me.'

She turned from watching the boys as they continued with their game. 'Why?'

He opened his mouth. He closed it again and rubbed the nape of his neck. 'I, uh… It wasn't very polite.'

'It wasn't impolite. You were obviously tired and needed the sleep.'

She selected an apple and crunched into it. 'Please eat something. It'll only go to waste and I hate that.'

He took a sandwich. Ham and pickle. 'Thank you.' And tried to remember the last time he'd let his guard down so comprehensively as to fall asleep when he hadn't meant to.

It certainly hadn't happened since Daniel had died.

His appetite fled. Nevertheless he forced himself to eat the sandwich. He wouldn't be able to stand the fuss his mother would make if he became ill. And this woman beside him had gone to the trouble of making these sandwiches for her children and herself and had chosen to share them with him. The least he could do was appreciate it.

He and Quinn sat side by side on the grass with their legs stretched out in front of them. They didn't speak much. A million questions pounded through him, but they were all far too personal and he had no right to ask a single one of them.

But the inactivity grated on him. It didn't seem to have that effect on Quinn, though. She lifted her face to the sky and closed her eyes as if relishing the sun and the day and the air. Eventually she jumped up again. 'I'm going to have another run with the boys for a bit. Stretch my legs. Feel free to join in.'

He glanced down at himself. 'I'm not exactly dressed for it.'

She took in his tie, his tailored trousers and polished leather shoes. 'No,' she agreed and he couldn't remember the last time he'd felt so summarily dismissed. 'Oh, I meant to tell you earlier that we're only going as far as Merredin today,' she shot over her shoulder before racing off towards the boys.

He looked Merredin up on his smart phone. A

quick calculation informed him it was only another two hours further on. Surely they could travel further than that in a day? He scowled and started answering email. He might as well do something useful. He made phone calls.

They stayed in Wundowie for another thirty minutes. He chafed to be away the entire time but was careful not to keep glancing at his watch. If they were only going as far as Merredin they'd be there mid-afternoon as it was. An additional half an hour in Wundowie either way wouldn't much matter.

Aidan would've liked to have kept working when they were back in the car, but he suspected Quinn would consider that bad manners.

He dragged a hand through his hair. What was he thinking? Of course it'd be bad manners. Besides, she and the boys had kept quiet so he could sleep and it hardly seemed fair to continue to expect such ongoing consideration. Especially when they were doing him a favour.

The fact his phone battery was running low decided it. He tucked it away and glanced around to the back seat. 'Do you boys play a sport?'

'Soccer,' said Robbie.

'Robbie is the best runner on his team,' Chase said.

Quinn glanced at him. 'He means fastest.'

Robbie's mouth turned down. 'I mightn't be in my new team.'

Quinn tensed. Aidan tried not to wince. He hadn't meant to tread into sensitive territory. 'Uh...' He searched for something to say.

'Do you play sport?' Robbie asked.

'Not any more.' And all of a sudden his heart felt heavy as a stone again.

'Why are you on the television?' Chase demanded to know. 'Mum said she'd seen you.'

'Because of my job. I'm a politician so I go on television to tell people how I'd run the country if they vote for me.'

Robbie frowned. 'Do you like your job?'

A bitter taste lined his mouth. 'Sure I do.'

'What do you do?'

'Well, I go into my office most days and I go to lots of meetings and...' Endless meetings. It took an effort of will to keep the tiredness out of his voice. 'I go on the television and talk on the radio and talk to newspaper reporters so they can tell all the people about the things I think would make our country run better. I have people who work for me and we draft up proposals for new policies.'

'Wouldn't being a fireman be more fun?'

'A fireman would be excellent fun,' he agreed. Lord, his mother would have a fit! He almost laughed.

'When you're finished being a politician maybe you could be a fireman,' Chase said.

'And then you could play soccer too,' added Robbie.

He didn't know how those two things were linked. He glanced at Quinn for direction. She merely smiled at him.

'Mum, can we play one of our CDs now?'

'I did promise the boys we'd play one of our CDs on this leg of our journey. We burned a few especially.'

'I don't mind.' It'd save him searching for topics of conversation.

'We sing pretty loud.'

'You don't need to apologise about that.'

For some reason that made her grin. 'You haven't heard our singing yet.'

He forced himself to smile.

She slipped a CD into the player. 'The Purple People-Eater' immediately blasted from the speakers and his three companions burst into loud accompaniment, the boys laughing throughout most of the song. That was followed by 'Llama Llama Duck' and then 'My Boomerang Won't Come Back'.

He stared at her. 'You have to be joking me?'

'Fun novelty songs are our favourite.' Her grin was so wide it almost split her face. 'If there's a doo-wop or chirpy-chirpy-cheep-cheep to be had then we love it.'

Hell, that was what this was. Absolute hell. He slunk down in his seat and stared straight out in front of him as the songs came at him in a relentless round. 'This isn't music!' He glared at the road. 'You could've warned me about this back in Perth.' No way would he have got into the car with her then.

Then he thought of his mother.

Quinn merely sang, 'I'm a yummy, tummy, funny, lucky gummy bear,' with extra gusto.

He closed his eyes, but this time sleep eluded him.

CHAPTER TWO

THEY REACHED MERREDIN ninety minutes later. It had felt like ninety hours. Aidan had endured forty minutes of the 'Monster Mash', 'Achy Breaky Heart' and many more novelty songs, which was enough to last him a lifetime. Twenty minutes of I Spy had followed and then a further thirty minutes of the number plate game. There was only one rule to the game, as far as he could tell, and that was who could make up the silliest phrase from the letters of a passing number plate.

PHH. Penguin haircuts here. Purple Hoovering hollyhocks. Pasta hates ham.

LSL. Larks sneeze loudly. Little snooty limpets. Lace scissored loquaciously.

CCC. Cream cake central. Can't clap cymbals. Cool cooler coolest.

And on and on and on it went, like some kind of slow Chinese water torture. His temples throbbed and an ache stretched behind his eyes. He didn't join in.

He sat up straighter though when Quinn eased the car down the town's main street. He glanced up at the sky. There was another four hours of daylight left yet. Another four hours of good driving time.

Manners prevented him from pointing this out. Biting back something less than charitable, he studied the few shops on offer. Maybe he'd be able to hire a car of his own out here?

Quinn parked the car in the main street and turned off the motor. 'The boys and I are staying at the caravan park, but I figured you'd be more comfortable at the motel.'

A caravan park? He suppressed a shudder. Again, he didn't say anything. Quinn was obviously on a tight budget.

She and the boys all but bounced out of the car. Aidan found his limbs heavy and lethargic. It took an effort of will to make them move. He wondered where Quinn found all her energy. Maybe she took vitamins. Unbidden, an image of her racing around the soccer oval in her bike shorts and dress rose up through him and for some reason his throat tightened.

He glanced up to find her watching him. He felt worn and weary, but her ponytail still bounced and her cheeks were pink and pretty. She waited, as if expecting him to say something, and then she merely shrugged. 'The motel is just across the road.' She pointed. 'We'll collect you at nine in the morning.'

He snapped to and retrieved his overnight bag from the back of the wagon. 'I'll be ready earlier. Say six or seven if you wanted to get an early start.'

'Nine o'clock,' she repeated, and he suddenly had the impression she was laughing at him.

She swung back to the boys. 'Right!' She clapped her hands. 'Chase, I need you to find me a packet of spaghetti and, Robbie, I need you to find me a tin of tomatoes.'

As they walked away he heard Chase ask, 'What are you looking for?'

'Minced meat and garlic bread.' And they all disappeared into the nearby supermarket.

He'd been summarily dismissed. Again.

From a grocery trip? He shook the thought off and headed across the road to the motel.

His room was adequate. Merredin might be the regional centre for Western Australia's wheat belt, but as far as he was concerned it wasn't much more than a two-horse town and his early enquiries about hiring a car proved less than encouraging.

He strode back to his motel room, set his phone to charge and then flipped open his laptop and searched Google Maps. He frowned. What the heck…? If they kept travelling at this pace it'd take them two weeks to drive across the country!

His hands clenched for a moment. Counting to three, he unclenched them and pulled a writing pad from his briefcase and started to plot a route across the continent. He spread out a map he'd grabbed from the motel's reception and marked logical break points where he and Quinn could swap driving duties.

That took all of twenty minutes. He closed his laptop and glanced about his room. There didn't seem to be much more to do. He wandered about the room, opening the wardrobe doors and the desk drawer. He made a coffee that he didn't drink. He reached for his cell phone to call his mother, stared at it for a moment and then shoved it back onto its charger.

Flopping back onto the bed, he stared at the ceiling for what seemed like an eon. When he glanced at his watch, though, he cursed. What on earth was he going to do for the rest of the afternoon, let alone the rest of the night?

He raised himself to his elbows. He could go and find Quinn and the boys.

Why would you do that?

He sat up and drummed his fingers against his thighs, before shooting to his feet. He tore the page from his writing pad and stalked from the room.

It didn't take him long to find the caravan park. And it didn't take him long to locate Robbie and Chase either. They played—somewhat rowdily—on a playground fort in primary colours so bright they hurt his eyes. And then he saw Quinn. She sat cross-legged on a blanket beside a nearby caravan, and something about her sitting in the afternoon light soothed his eyes.

'Hey, Aidan,' she called out when she saw him. 'Feeling at a loose end, huh?'

He rolled his shoulders. 'I'm just exploring. Thought I'd come see where you were camped.'

She lifted her face to the sun. 'This is a nice spot, isn't it?'

It was? He glanced around, searching for whatever it was that she found 'nice', but he came up blank.

'I thought you'd be busy catching up on all of your work.'

It hit him that in amongst all of his restlessness it hadn't occurred to him to ring back into the office. They knew he was delayed, but…

It didn't mean he had to stop working. There'd still be the usual endless round of email that needed answering. He could've set up meetings for this evening on Skype.

The thought of all that work made him feel as tired as the idea of ringing his mother. When Quinn gestured to the blanket he fell down onto it, grateful for the respite.

He had no right feeling so exhausted. He'd done next to nothing all day. He shook himself in an effort to keep the moroseness at bay, glanced around as if he were curious about his surroundings. If he pretended well enough, maybe he'd start to feel a flicker of interest and intent again. Maybe. 'Are you planning to stay in caravan parks for all of your journey?'

'You bet.'

He kept his face smooth, but somehow she saw through him and threw her head back with a laugh. 'Not your idea of a good time, I see.'

'I wouldn't say that.' He wasn't a snob, but…

Walking to an amenity block when he could have an en suite bathroom? No, thanks.

'Only because you're incredibly polite.'

She made that sound like an insult.

'Look about you, Aidan. This place caters to children far better than your motel does. Most caravan parks do. Look at all that open green space over there. The boys can kick a ball around to their hearts' content. And then there's that playground, which I might add is fenced.'

In those eye-gouging primary colours.

'Robbie is old enough not to wander off, but Chase is still easily distracted.'

He straightened when he realised this place gave her peace of mind. 'I hadn't thought of that.'

'And there're usually other children around for them to play with too.'

He watched another two children approach the playground.

'Most people here won't mind a bit of noise from the children, but I bet you're glad we're not staying in the room next to yours at the motel.'

He rolled his shoulders. 'It's not a bad noise. It's just a bit of laughing and shouting.'

She raised her eyebrows.

'But I take your point.'

'It'd be hard to get any work done with all that noise.'

There she was, talking about work again.

He promptly pulled the itinerary he'd plotted out for them from his pocket along with the map and smoothed them on the rug between them. 'I thought that tomorrow we could make it as far as Balladonia. If we wanted to take two-hour shifts driving, which is what all the driver reviver and driving safety courses recommend, then we could change here, here and here.' He pointed out the various locations on the map.

Quinn leaned back on her hands and laughed. 'I've seen this movie. In this particular scenario you're Sally and I'm Harry, right?'

He stared at her. What on earth was she talking about?

'*When Harry Met Sally*,' she said when he remained silent. 'The movie? You know? Sally who's a bit uptight and super-organised and Harry who's casual and laidback?'

He searched for something to say.

'There's a scene early in the movie when they're driving across America together and...' Her voice lost steam. 'You haven't seen the movie?'

He shook his head.

Her face fell. 'But it's one of the classic rom-coms of all time.'

For some reason he felt compelled to apologise. 'I'm sorry.'

And for some reason he couldn't fathom that made her smile again, only it wasn't the kind of smile that reached her eyes. She touched his map and shook her head. 'No.'

He blinked. 'No?' But...

She laughed and he could see it was partly in frustration with him, but she didn't do it in a mean way. She rested back on her hands again. 'Aidan, you really need to learn to relax and chill out a bit.'

And just like that she reminded him of Daniel.

It should've hurt him.

But it didn't.

'I...'

He stared at her as if he'd never seen her before. Or as if no one had ever told him to slow down and smell the roses. He stared at her as if that very concept was totally alien.

She bit back a sigh. This trip—spending time with her boys and doing all she could to make this transition in their lives exciting and easy—was important to her. Taking pity on Aidan and inviting him to join them had thrown the dynamic off more than she'd anticipated. She'd promised the boys a holiday and she wasn't going back on her word.

And eight hours a day driving wasn't a holiday in anybody's vocabulary.

'We probably should've compared notes about the kind of travelling we were expecting to do before we left Perth.' How could he know she meant to take it slow if she hadn't explained it to him? He was obviously in a hurry, but... 'It didn't occur to me at the time.' She moistened her lips. 'But we're obviously working on two different timetables here.'

Her stomach churned. He was probably used to everyone rushing around at a million miles an hour. That was what people from his world—her parents' world—did.

Don't hold that against him. It doesn't make him like your parents.

'I made enquiries in town to see if I could hire a car of my own.'

She swallowed. It'd be one solution to the problem. 'And?'

'No luck, I'm afraid.'

'I see.'

'You're regretting taking me on as a passenger.' He said it simply, without rancour, but there was such exhaustion stretching through his voice it was all she could do to not reach across and clasp his hand and to tell him he was mistaken. Only...

She glanced across at her boys, now happily playing with the newcomers to the playground. A fierce mixture of love and fear swirled through her. Pushing her shoulders back, she met his stare again. Pussyfooting around would only lead to more misunderstandings. 'Aidan, you've been unfailingly polite, but you haven't really been all that friendly.'

'I beg your pardon?'

He gritted his teeth so hard his mouth turned white. She hated being the reason for that expression, but she soldiered on all the same, hoping she wasn't punishing him for the reminders of the past that he'd unwittingly brought rushing back to her. 'You didn't join in on our singalong. You didn't play I Spy or the number plate game.'

He stared at her. For someone groomed to project and maintain a certain image, he looked all at sea. 'Please don't tell me you want to part company here in this two-horse town.'

'Of course not!' How could he think she'd abandon him like that?

'Once we reach Adelaide I'll make other arrangements.'

'Okay.' She bit her thumbnail for a moment,
unable to look at him. Adelaide was still six or
possibly seven days away yet. If she could make
him see how important this trip was...well, then,
he might make more of an effort to fit in. Maybe.

She stretched her legs out in front of her. 'You
know what I think? I think we should break the
ice a little. I think we should ask the questions
that have been itching through us and get that all
out of the way.'

He looked so utterly appalled she had to bite
her lip to stop from laughing. This man took self-
contained to a whole new level. 'Or, better yet,
why don't we tell each other something we think
the other wants to know?'

His expression didn't change but she ignored
it to clap her hands. 'Yes, that'll be much more
fun. I'll go first, shall I?' she rushed on before
he could object. She crossed her legs again. 'I'm
going to tell you why Robbie, Chase and I are on
a road trip across the continent.'

He shifted, grew more alert. She could tell from

the way his eyes focused on her and his shoulders straightened. Oh, he was appalled still, of course, but she hoped his curiosity would eventually conquer his resistance.

'The olive farm is in the Hunter Valley wine district and it belongs to my aunt. She's the black sheep of the family.' She rolled her eyes. 'And I happen to take after her.'

'Your family consider you a black sheep?'

A question! She schooled her features to hide her triumph. 'Actually, in all honesty, I'd be very surprised if my parents thought about me at all these days. They're from Sydney. I became pregnant with Robbie when I was eighteen. They wanted me to go to university and carve out some mythically brilliant career. When I decided to have my baby instead, they cut me off.'

His jaw dropped. He mightn't be 'friendly' in a traditional sense, but he didn't strike her as the kind of man who'd walk away from his family when they needed him.

And you're basing that on what—his pretty smiles and earnest eyes in his television interviews?

Hmm, good point.

'Siblings?'

Another question! 'None. So, after my parents handed me their ultimatum, I packed my bags and moved to Perth.'

'Why Perth?'

'Because it was about as far away from Sydney as I could get while still remaining in the country.'

He stared at her for a long moment. She held her breath and crossed her fingers that he'd ask a fourth question.

'Did Robbie's father go with you?'

She wanted to beam at him for asking. 'Yes, he did.' But she didn't want to tell him that story. 'When I had Robbie my Aunt Mara—'

'Of black sheep fame?'

He was totally hooked, whether he knew it or not. 'The very one. Well, she came across to Perth to help me out for a couple of weeks. I was barely nineteen with a new baby. I appreciated every bit of help, advice and support she gave me.'

He plucked a nearby dandelion. 'That's nice.'

'She didn't have to. We'd had very little to do with each other when I was growing up.' Her parents had made sure of that. 'But those two weeks bonded us together in a way I will always cherish. We've been close ever since.'

'You're moving to be nearer to her?'

A little twist of fear burrowed into her gut. She shifted on the blanket. She was turning all of their lives upside down. What if she was making a mistake? They'd had a perfectly comfortable life in Perth.

You weren't happy.

Her happiness had nothing to do with it. She scratched her nose and stared across at Robbie and Chase.

'Quinn?'

She shook herself and pasted on a smile. 'Mara is only fifty-two but she's developed severe arthritis. She needs a hip replacement.' She needed help. 'My boys don't have any family in Perth. I think it'd be nice for them to know Mara better.'

Comprehension flashed across his face. 'You're moving there to look after her.'

'I expect we'll all look after each other. Like I said, she owns an olive farm and her second-in-command recently married and moved to the States.'

'And you're going to fill the position?'

He didn't ask with any judgement in his voice. She shouldn't feel as if she'd been found so... lacking. 'Yes.'

She tossed her head. Besides, she was looking forward to that challenge. Her admin job in the Department of Chemistry at the University of Western Australia had palled years ago. Not that it had ever had much shine.

Still, it had provided them with the security of a fortnightly pay packet. It had supported her and the boys for the last five years. It—

She slammed a halt on the doubts that tried to crowd her. If worse came to worse, if things didn't work out at Aunt Mara's, she'd be able to pick up an office job in no time at all. Somewhere.

She bit back a sigh and then straightened her spine. There was absolutely no reason why things wouldn't work out. She loved her aunt. So did the boys. The Hunter Valley was a beautiful place and the boys would thrive in all of that sunshine and the wide open spaces. They'd go to good schools and she'd get them a dog. They'd make friends fast. And so would she.

She crossed her fingers. The change might even help her overcome the ennui that had started to take her over. She'd learn new skills and maybe, eventually, she'd stop feeling so alone.

Win-win for everyone. Perfect!

She turned back to Aidan and pressed her hands together. 'This is such an exciting time for us.'

'And a scary one too, I imagine.'

She didn't want to admit that. Not out loud.

'I mean you're turning your whole life on its head.'

She sucked her bottom lip into her mouth and concentrated on keeping her breathing even.

He stared across at the playground. 'And it's not just your life that this decision impacts either so—'

'Are you trying to make me hyperventilate?' she demanded.

His jaw dropped. 'Heck, no! I just think it's amazing and courageous and...'

She gritted her teeth for a moment before pasting on another smile. She suspected it was more a grimace from the way Aidan eased back a fraction and kept his eyes trained on her. 'Which is why this road trip of ours is so important to me. I've promised the boys that we'll treat it as a holiday. I'm determined that we'll take our time and that everyone will be as relaxed as possible so I can answer any questions about this new life of ours, help ease any fears and apprehensions that might come to light, and to just...'

She reached out as if to grasp the words she sought from the air. 'To help us all look forward to this new beginning and be excited about it.' She turned to him, willing him to understand. 'It's the reason I've been chirpy-chirpy-cheeping with all of my might.'

Beneath his tan, he paled. 'And I'm screwing that up for you.'

'No you're not. Not exactly. But now that you know, maybe you can ease up a bit.'

'And part company with you at Adelaide.'

She slapped a hand down on the blanket between them and leaned in closer. He smelled of something spicy and sharp like eucalyptus oil or crushed pine needles. She breathed him in and the constriction about her lungs eased a fraction. 'By going with the flow and relaxing,' she corrected. 'You're obviously stressed about this plane strike and getting back home to Sydney, but…'

He latched onto that. 'But?'

'We're all stuck with each other for the six days or so, right?'

'Six days!' He swallowed. He nodded. 'Six days. Right.'

'So can't you stop chafing at the constraints

and just…just look at this time as a bit of a gift? Embrace it as an unexpected holiday or a time-out from a hectic schedule?'

He stared at her. 'A holiday?' He said the words as if testing them out. Very slowly he started to nod. 'Fretting about the delay isn't going to change anything, is it?'

Precisely.

'In fact, it would be making things harder on you and the boys.'

'And on you.' She shook her head. 'I hate to think what your raised cortisol levels are doing to your overall heath.'

'Cortisol?'

'It's a hormone that's released into our bloodstreams during times of stress. It's not good for us in large constant doses.' It took an effort of will not to fidget under his stare. She waved a dismissive hand. 'I read about it in a book.'

This man would benefit from regular meditation too, but she didn't suggest it. She'd suggested enough for one day. She leant back on her hands and lifted her face to what was left of the sun and made herself laugh. 'We're certainly getting holiday weather.' Summer might be over officially, but nobody had informed the weather of that fact.

He glanced around and nodded.

'Look at how blue the sky is and the golden haze on the horizon. This is my absolute favourite time of day.'

His shoulders loosened.

'I love the way the shadows lengthen and how stands of trees almost turn purple in the shade, like those ones over there,' she murmured.

He pulled in an audible breath and let it out in one long exhalation.

'I just want to drink it all in.'

They were quiet for a few moments. She hoped he was savouring the afternoon as much as she was.

'You remind me of someone.'

It was the most relaxed she'd heard him sound. 'Who?'

He swivelled to face her. 'My turn.'

She blinked. 'For?'

'For sharing something I think you want to know.'

It took all her willpower to not lean forward, mouth agape. She hadn't expected him to actually take part in her 'you tell me yours, I'll tell you mine' strategy. She'd just wanted to impress upon him the importance of this trip. Not that she had any intention of telling him that now, though.

'Okay.' She forced her eyes back to the hazy horizon, careful to not make him feel self-conscious.

'Daniel's death has devastated my family.'

His brother had died in a car accident eight months ago now. It had made all the headlines. She gripped a fistful of blanket, her heart burning for Aidan and his family.

'He was the apple of my parents' eyes. His death shattered them.' He stared down at his hands. 'Hardly surprising as he was a great guy.'

He didn't have to say how much his brother's death had devastated him. She could see it in his face. A lump ballooned in her throat.

'Ever since Danny's accident my mother has lived in mortal fear of losing me too.'

The poor woman.

And then Quinn saw it, what Aidan wasn't saying. With an effort, she swallowed and the lump bruised her all the way down until it reached her stomach. 'So this plane strike and your road trip across the country, it's going to be a real…worry for her?'

And that was what had really been chafing at him. Not the interruption to his political campaigning or the fact he was missing important meetings.

'What did you call it? Cortisol?'

She nodded.

He pointed skyward. 'Hers will be through the roof.'

And Aidan wanted to do whatever he could to ease his mother's suffering. Her heart tore for him.

'My parents' thirtieth wedding anniversary is soon and—'

'When?' Good Lord! She had to make sure he got home in time for that.

'Not until the twenty-fourth of the month.'

She let out a breath. She was hoping to be at Mara's no later than the twenty-second. He'd get home in time.

'I should be there helping with all the preparations. There's a huge party planned. I encouraged them to have it. I thought it might help.'

That was when she started to wonder how much of his life he was putting on hold in an effort to allay his parents' grief. And what of his own grief?

She surveyed him for a long moment. When he turned to meet her gaze the rich brown of his eyes almost stole her breath. She swallowed, but she didn't look away. 'Aidan, I am truly sorry for your loss.'

He looked ragged for a moment. 'Thank you.'

The silence gathered about them and started to burn. 'May I say something about your mother?' she whispered.

He stilled. He turned back. 'Only if you say it gently.'

Gently? Her heart started to thump. She moistened her lips and stared across to the playground with its riot of happy laughter. 'I can't imagine how bad it would be to lose one of my boys.' Her voice wobbled. 'I can't actually imagine anything worse.'

He reached out and squeezed her hand.

'In fact, I can't actually comprehend it, and I'm utterly and probably somewhat selfishly grateful for that.'

'It's not selfish, Quinn,' he said quietly.

'Your poor, *poor* mother, Aidan.' She clasped his hand tightly. 'God forbid if I should ever lose

Robbie, but… I can't help feeling that wrapping Chase up in cotton wool would not be a good thing to do. For him or for me.'

He met her gaze, his face sober. 'She can't help her grief.'

'No.' But tying Aidan down like this was hardly fair. 'You will get home safe and sound and in one piece.' It was probably a foolish thing to say because neither one of them could guarantee that. But she couldn't think of anything else to say.

'Of course I will.'

'And there's nothing you can do for your mother at the moment except to give her a daily phone call to let her know you're okay.'

'No,' he agreed.

'Can you live with that?'

'I guess I'll have to.'

'You know,' she started slowly, 'this might be a good thing.'

'How?'

'Maybe it'll force her to focus beyond her fear, especially if she has the party to turn her attention to. And once she does that she might realise how irrational her fear is.'

His face lit up. 'You think so?'

Oh, heavens, she'd raised his hopes. Um...
'Maybe.'

He stared at her for a long moment and then he
smiled. 'That person you remind me of?'

Her heart started to thump. 'Uh-huh?'

'It's Daniel. Quinn, you remind me of my
brother.'

CHAPTER THREE

AIDAN TOOK THE first driving shift the next day. He'd thought he might have an argument on his hands about that but, after subjecting him to a thorough scrutiny, Quinn merely handed him the keys and slid into the passenger seat.

He surveyed her the best he could without alerting her to that fact. She looked a little pale, a little wan.

'Okay, boys.' She turned to Robbie and Chase in the back. 'You have one hour of Gameboy time.'

Both boys whooped and dived into their backpacks. She shrugged when she caught Aidan's eye. 'I know it'd make things a whole lot easier and simpler, not to mention quieter, if I just let them play with their Gameboys all day, but I don't think that's good for them.'

'I don't either.'

Her brows shot up. 'It's something you've thought about?'

He might not have kids, he might not really know any kids, but it didn't make him totally ignorant. 'Only in the abstract.' Besides, he hoped to have kids one day. 'The rise in childhood obesity is worrying. I've been part of a government task force that's been looking at strategies to combat it.'

'That's good to know.' Yesterday she'd have asked him all sorts of questions about it. Today she stifled a yawn and stared out of the window with a mumbled, 'Glad our taxes are being put to good use.'

Aidan had set their course on the Great Eastern Highway and the scenery grew browner and drier by the kilometre. All that was visible from the windows was low scrub, brown grass and brown dirt. For mile upon endless mile.

He glanced across at her again. 'Rough night?'

She straightened and he wished he'd kept quiet and just let her drift off for a little while.

'The bed was hard as a rock.'

She smiled but it left him vaguely dissatisfied. Quinn might spout assurances that this move across the country was the greatest idea ever, but he sensed a certain ambivalence in her.

That she doesn't want to talk about.

Yesterday's disclosures didn't give him the right to pry.

'I'll sleep very well tonight, though.' She sent him one of her buck-up smiles. 'Whether the bed is made of rock or marshmallow.'

He determined in that moment to let her rest as much as he could. 'Mind if I turn on the radio? I'll keep the volume low.'

'Sounds nice.'

Although he willed her to, she didn't fall asleep. She merely stared out of the window and watched the unending scrub pass by. At the one hour mark she snapped to and turned to the boys. 'Time's up.'

There were groans and grumbles and 'let me just finish this bit' but within five minutes they'd tucked their Gameboys back into their bags. Quinn then asked them what games they'd been playing and received blow-by-blow accounts. She spoke her children's lingo. She connected with them on every level and he suddenly and deeply admired her.

She was a single working mother, but she'd evidently spent time building a solid relationship with her children. It couldn't have been easy, she'd have had to make sacrifices, but he suspected she hadn't minded that in the least.

Robbie stretched out his arms to touch the back of Aidan's seat. 'How long is Aunt Mara going to be in hospital for?'

'If all goes well, just a few days. But she'll have to take it easy for weeks and weeks. Don't forget, though, that her surgery isn't scheduled until later in the year.'

'I'll read to her.'

'She'll like that.'

'And I'll play cars with her,' Chase piped up, evidently not wanting to be left out.

'Heavens! She'll be back on her feet in no time with all of that attention.'

Robbie stretched to touch the roof. 'What are we going to do for a car if we have to give this one back?'

'We're going to share Aunt Mara's car for a while and there's a farm ute we can use too. But we'll buy a new one eventually. What do you guys think we should get?'

A lively discussion followed, mostly based on television ads that the boys liked. It made Aidan smile. And then he remembered Quinn's words of yesterday and how she'd thought him unfriendly and the smile slid straight off his face. He had to do more than just listen. 'What about a minivan?' he suggested. 'One of those bus things that can practically carry an entire football team.'

The boys thought that a brilliant idea. Quinn accused him of harbouring a secret desire for a shed on wheels, which made him laugh.

'So,' he asked when silence reigned again, 'are you boys looking forward to the move?'

'Yes,' said Chase without hesitation.

In the rear-view mirror he saw Robbie frown and chew the side of his thumb. 'I'm going to miss my friends Luke and Jason.'

Quinn's hands clenched. He flicked a glance at them before turning his attention back to the road. 'I know it's not precisely the same, but you'll be able to Skype with them, won't you?'

Robbie frowned more fiercely. 'What's that?'

'It's like talking on the phone only on the computer, and you get to see each other.'

He stopped chewing his thumb. 'Really?' His face lit up. 'Can I, Mum? Huh, can I?'

Quinn's hands unclenched. 'Sure you can, honey.'

She sent Aidan such a smile he was tempted to simply sit back and bask in it. But then he remembered yesterday's impression. Unfriendly? He wasn't having a bit of it.

'And can I Skype with Daddy too?'

He swore every single muscle Quinn possessed bunched at that. 'I...' She cleared her throat. 'I don't see why not.' She flashed Robbie a smile. For some reason it made Aidan want to drop his head to the steering wheel. He kept both hands tight about it, though, and his eyes glued to the road ahead. 'You'll have to ask him the next time he rings.'

''Kay.'

'Look, kangaroos!' Aidan hollered, pointing to the right and blessing Providence for providing them with the perfect distraction.

Both boys strained in their seats, their mouths open and their faces eager as they watched four large grey kangaroos bounce through the scrub beside the car.

Quinn leant her head back against the seat and closed her eyes.

Aidan pulled in a breath. 'Okay, Robbie and Chase, I think it's time I taught you a song.'

'Is it a fun song?' Chase demanded, as if that was the only kind of song he was interested in.

He scrubbed a hand across his chin. 'It has a yellow submarine. Does that make it fun enough?'

'Yes!' the boys chorused.

Besides, it was a classic. If they were all so hell-bent on novelty songs they might as well learn the best. So he taught them the Beatles' 'Yellow Submarine'. By the time they'd finished they'd reached their first rest stop. While Quinn spread out the picnic blanket in the park area behind the lone roadhouse, Aidan grabbed his laptop and downloaded the song so the boys could listen to the original version. The three of them sang along at the tops of their voices.

When they'd finished, Aidan turned to find Quinn curled on the blanket, fast asleep. He thought of his exhaustion of the previous day. He thought about how she was turning her whole world on its head. He swung back to the boys. 'How about we kick a ball around and let your mum sleep?'

'I'm tired of kicking a ball around,' Chase grumbled. 'I wanna play hopscotch instead.'

Hopscotch?

Without a murmur, Robbie went to the boot of the car and pulled out a plastic mat which, when unfolded, formed a life-sized hopscotch…court, shape or whatever one called it.

'Uh, guys…' Aidan glanced at Quinn. He shook his head. 'Never mind.'

So they played hopscotch.

And darn if it wasn't fun!

'Are you guys worried about making friends in your new home town?'

Chase hopped. 'Mum said it'll be really easy to make friends in school.'

'I expect she's right.' Aiden patted Chase's back. 'Well done, buddy; that was a big hop to end with.'

Robbie took his turn. 'Mum said I can play Saturday morning soccer in Pokolbin, just like I did in Perth.'

'Sport is a great way to make friends.' He stepped back to give Robbie plenty of room to finish his turn. 'You're quick at this.'

'I know.' Robbie nodded, but as Aidan took his turn he could tell the boy was pleased with the praise.

'You'd be quicker if you had play clothes.'

Aidan puffed over the finish line. 'Ain't that the truth? I'll have to buy some when we get to Norseman this afternoon.'

Robbie squinted up at Aidan, chewing his lip. Aidan mightn't have a kid of his own, he mightn't have friends with kids, but it didn't take a rocket scientist to work out that Robbie had something he wanted to ask. 'Out with it, buddy,' he advised.

'You gotta promise to tell me the truth.'

Jeez! He rubbed a hand across his jaw. 'I'll do my best.'

'Is hopscotch a girls' game?'

Aidan automatically went to say no, that anyone was at liberty to play hopscotch, which wasn't really a lie, but… He closed his mouth. Kids could be cruel and, as far as he could tell, political correctness wasn't high on their radar, regardless of what their parents tried to teach them.

He squatted down in front of Robbie and Chase, a glance over his shoulder confirming that Quinn still slept. 'Okay, it shouldn't just be a girls' game, but it kinda is.' He didn't want these kids getting bullied. 'So I wouldn't play it at your new school.'

'Right.' Robbie nodded, evidently glad the question had been settled.

Chase leant against Aidan and the rush of the child's heat against his arm did something strange to Aidan's stomach. He had a sudden primeval impulse to take out anyone who tried to hurt these kids.

'But,' Chase whispered, 'I like playing hopscotch.'

And nobody should be allowed to prevent these kids from enjoying such an innocent diversion. 'That's why I think you should play it at home whenever you want. If anyone finds out about it and gives you a hard time, tell them your mum makes you play it with her. In fact—' a grin built through him '—when you have friends around, tee up with your mum beforehand to make you all play it.'

They'd all love it. He'd tell Quinn to make cake…or chocolate crackles. Kids would forgive any eccentricity for chocolate crackles. They might groan to their parents or other kids that Ms Laverty made them play hopscotch, but then they'd remember the chocolate crackles and still think she was great.

It'd be a win all round.

He beamed at the boys. They beamed back. 'C'mon, who's up next?'

Quinn woke to find Aidan playing hopscotch with Robbie and Chase. She blinked. She sat up and then had to blink again. He actually looked as if he was having fun!

She suddenly grinned, all trace of her thundering headache gone. The sun, the clear blue sky and the dry dusty smells of the rest area seemed filled with a promise they'd all lacked earlier.

She lifted her chin and pushed away the doubts that had spent the night harrying and hounding her. This new beginning should be savoured, not dreaded. Mindless worrying wouldn't help any of them.

Aidan glanced around as if he'd sensed her gaze. Her heart did a silly little flip-flop. Actually, maybe it wasn't so silly. Perhaps it was entirely understandable. Aidan looked a whole lot more…uh, personable without his jacket and tie…or his shoes and socks.

'You lot must be ready for a drink and a snack,' she called out, but her voice came out a bit higher and threadier than it usually did. She blamed it on the dust in the air. The boys raced over, full of reports of their game, but she only heard every second word. Her eyes never left Aidan. He packed up the game and then ambled over—practically sauntering—and it highlighted the leanness of his hips and the power of his thighs.

And it made her throat as dry as a desert. An ancient hunger built through her. Ancient as in primeval. And ancient as in she hadn't experienced this kind of hunger in over five years. She dragged her gaze away, refused to let it dwell on a body that interested her far too much. Bodies were just bodies. Hormones were just hormones. And this was nothing more than a hormone-induced aberration. She handed out sliced apple, carrot sticks and bottled water and kept her eyes to herself as best she could.

Aidan fell down onto the blanket beside her, slugging her with his heat. The scent of his perspiration rose up, making her gulp. She tried telling herself she loathed man sweat. But it was clean sweat earned in the service of playing with her children and she couldn't hate it. Beneath it threaded that woodsy spice that she'd like to get to know a whole lot better.

'How are you feeling?'

His words rumbled against her. She grabbed an apple slice and crunched it, nodding her head all the while. 'Much better. Thank you for letting me sleep—' she glanced at her watch '—for a whole hour!' He'd taken care of the boys for a whole hour? 'Oh my word! What kind of irresponsible mother you must think me!' What kind of mother just fell asleep in a strange place and—?

'I think you're a brilliant mother, Quinn.'

She had to look at him then. Her mouth opened and closed but no sound came out.

'So do we,' Robbie said.

Chase nodded.

She had to swallow a lump. 'Thank you.' She cleared her throat. 'All of you.'

'I'm going to run now,' Robbie said gravely, and then proceeded to do precisely that. Chase followed at his heels.

She turned back to Aidan to find those molten amber eyes surveying her. 'Thank you for keeping them entertained.'

'It was no big deal.'

He lifted a shoulder, which only alerted her to the fact that while he might not have the physique of a bodybuilder, his shoulders had breadth and his chest didn't lack for depth.

Oh, stop it. She dug fingernails into her palms. A man let her sleep for an hour and she became a sex maniac? *I don't think so.*

'The boys and I had fun. You obviously didn't sleep well last night and I expect the last few weeks have been hectic with the preparations for the move. You're entitled to some downtime too.'

And for the first time in a long time she caught a glimpse of what it must be like to co-parent rather than having to do it all on her own. The vision was unbelievably beguiling.

A man let her sleep for an hour so she built family fantasies about him? She bit back a snort. *I don't think so.* Those fantasies were nothing but a big fat lie. In her experience, most men couldn't be trusted to stick to something as important as fatherhood and even if Aidan proved to be one of the exceptions he never would with her.

And she sure as heck wouldn't with him! Nothing—*nothing*—would ever induce her back into his world and that privileged circle again. She could see it already—the claims of his job would eventually take precedence over his wife and any children he might have. In effect, his wife would be a single parent. Mind you, she'd have the money to hire nannies, but what were nannies to a parent's love? Quinn refused to raise her children in a world where social status and professional prestige were more important than the warmth and intimacy of family ties.

She bit into another slice of apple and glared at

a nearby stunted tree, grateful Aidan hadn't connected her with the Sydney Lavertys. It wasn't something she publicised and it certainly wasn't something she wanted to talk about.

But the memory of his world brought her back to herself. It reminded her of all of his responsibilities and duties. 'How was your mother when you rang her last night?'

He grimaced.

This was one of the many things she'd considered in the wee small hours when sleep had refused to come. 'I thought about her last night.'

He lifted a brow. 'And?'

'I think you need to give her a task, something concrete to do.'

'To take her mind off...other things?'

'It's hard to brood when you're busy.'

He considered her words and very slowly the line around his mouth eased. 'I could get her to double check the arrangements with the caterers and—'

'I was thinking—'

She broke off and flushed. 'Sorry, that was rude of me. I have no right stomping on your ideas with my big fat hypothetical work boots.'

'I'd like to hear your idea.'

He would? She glanced up to find him watching her closely and it occurred to her that he wouldn't have been nearly as open if he'd known her. But as they'd never clap eyes on each other again—well, she might see him on the television but that didn't count—after the next few days it was almost as if they were in a bubble. A bubble that had no impact or relevance on their real day-to-day lives. And when they returned to those real lives there'd be barely a ripple of this time to ruffle the surface.

It was unbelievably freeing. She understood that.

It was also unutterably sad, which she didn't understand at all.

She shrugged that off and dragged her attention back to the conversation. 'I just think you need to give your mother something to do that she can't shrug off as unimportant or that she can delegate to someone else.'

'You think she considers the party unimportant?'

Yikes! She'd need to tread carefully. Aidan had been through enough and she had no wish to hurt his feelings. Before she could roll out a tactful response, though, he said, 'You think the party is making me feel better, but not my mother.'

'I don't know your mother, Aidan, so I can't possibly comment on that.' He leaned away from her. Lines of strain fanned out from his mouth and it made her heart clench. 'I bet it's making your father feel better.'

His head snapped up, confirming her suspicions. She made herself smile. 'And that's no mean feat, surely?' The man had lost his child too.

Air rushed out of him. 'Dad and I concocted the party idea between us.' He lifted a hand as if to push it back through his hair, but he let it drop as if he didn't have the energy for it. 'It's given us something else to focus on.'

Her heart thumped. 'Aidan?'

He looked up.

'A party, no matter how ritzy and beautiful, or how well-meaning, won't...'

'Won't make up to my mother for losing a son,' he said, blunt and emotionless.

She tried not to flinch.

'You must think I'm an unbelievable idiot, and shallow to boot, to think a party would help.'

'I think you're worried about your mother and want to see her happy.'

He met her eyes.

'But I think you might be better served giving her something to do that *she* thinks is important. I mean as important as your desire to cheer her up is to you.'

He mulled her suggestion over for a moment. She could see his mind ticking over, but she had no idea what conclusion he came to. 'You make a good case.' The faintest of smiles touched his lips and something inside her unclenched a fraction. 'I take it you have had a thought or two on that head as well.'

'Well…yes.'

The smile grew a millimetre or two bigger. 'C'mon then, out with it.'

She pulled in a breath. 'I asked myself what your mother would consider important and I didn't have to go far to find it—you. She's invested in your happiness and your welfare, yes?'

His lips twisted. 'Yes.'

'Therefore, I expect your career is of prime importance to her.'

He closed his eyes and just like that any trace of a smile vanished. Her throat tightened as if a fist squeezed about it. She wasn't sure what she'd said wrong, but she had no intention of adding to her travelling companion's heartache. She straightened and eased back. 'I'm sorry. Like I said before, this is none of my business and I have no right—'

'I would like to hear what you have to say.'

She bit her lip but his gaze held hers so steadily that eventually she nodded. 'I was thinking that you should ask her to go into your office to oversee the daily operations of your campaign while you're not there.'

'I have staff to do that!'

'You could tell her that you respect your staff, but that you trust her rather than them to have your best interests at heart.' She rubbed her right hand back and forth across her left. 'You could tell her that you believe she was one of the reasons your father was elected when he ran for office back in the nineties. You could tell her that if she can find the time and has the heart for it, that it would mean the world to you if she would help you run your campaign.'

He'd gone grey. 'It's the one thing I've been avoiding.'

She bit her lip but the question slipped out anyway. 'Why?'

He stared up at the sky for a long moment. 'Selfish reasons.'

She bit her lip so hard then that nothing could slip out.

He straightened and pushed his shoulders back. 'You're right, though. That's precisely the kind of thing that would give her another focus. Dad and I have been wrapping her in cotton wool and that's the last thing she needs right now. What she needs is to be busy with some project close to her heart.'

'It's not selfish to want to protect the people we love. It's natural.'

He reached out to grip her shoulder, squeeze it, but his smile didn't reach his eyes. 'You're wise beyond your years. Thank you.'

She frowned. 'You're welcome.'

His hand remained on her shoulder and every nerve in her body sprang to life, making her breath hitch. He stilled and then his gaze speared to hers. He took in the expression on her face and that hot caramel gaze of his lowered to her lips. Something inside her started to tremble and gasp and her blood quickened in a sweet rush of need.

His eyes darkened. Hunger flared in their depths. His gaze locked to hers. 'Quinn?' He leaned towards her.

She tried to shake her head, to negate the question in his eyes, but her body refused to cooperate with her common sense. Her lips parted. If she leaned towards him...

A stream of childhood laughter reached her and it gave her just enough strength to close her eyes and lower her chin. Aidan removed his hand and eased back, but his scent—all spice and woods— wove around her, and she started to ache. She heard him climb to his feet. If she just whispered his name...

'Probably time for us to hit the road again.'

She snapped her eyes open and steeled her spine. She gave a swift nod of agreement. Excellent idea. She didn't say the words out loud, though. She didn't trust her voice not to betray her.

They reached Norseman at five o'clock.

Norseman had a population of sixteen hundred and was one of the few towns on the Nullarbor Plain with decent facilities. Quinn had called ahead to book her and the boys a caravan for the night. Tonight, regardless of how hard her bunk might prove to be, she'd be asleep by the time her head hit the pillow.

She and the boys had hamburgers for dinner. She allayed her guilt by telling herself they were on their holidays.

She didn't know where Aidan ate. Or when. Her efforts to avoid him had met with spectacular success. She suspected that was due to the fact that she had his full cooperation on that front.

She thought of that moment again—the moment when they might have kissed—and her breath jammed. How much she'd wanted to kiss him! But kissing Aidan was out of the question. The world he belonged to had betrayed her before. She wasn't giving it a chance to hurt her again.

Thank heavens for Robbie and Chase. They kept her busy, claiming most of her attention and giving her little time to brood. However, they both fell asleep before seven o'clock. Quinn might be tired, but seven o'clock was far too early for a grown woman to go to bed.

She glanced around the caravan, rubbed her hands together a few times, picked up a magazine and then put it down again. She was too wired.

With a glance at the sleeping boys, she eased the door to their caravan open and slipped outside. If the insects weren't too fierce she could sit out here at one of the picnic tables for a bit and lap up the quiet.

And the quiet was amazing. So was the dark. It had never been this dark in her suburb in Perth. She glanced up and her jaw dropped. She took a few steps forward. Stars, magnificent in their brightness and multitude, stretched across a navy dark sky and she wasn't sure she'd ever seen anything so spectacular in all her life.

'It takes your breath away, doesn't it?'

Aidan! She half turned but kept her gaze firmly fixed on the stars. *He* stole her breath. 'They're amazing.' And if her breath came out a tad husky she'd blame it on the night air and the majesty of the sky.

'I was hoping you'd be out here.'

That made her look at him.

He held a bottle of wine in one hand and two wine glasses in the other. Her mouth dried. 'Aidan,' she croaked. 'I—'

'It's just a glass of wine, Quinn. That's all, I promise.'

Without another word, she took a seat at the

table he gestured to and accepted a glass of wine with a murmured, 'Thank you.' She couldn't help it. There was something about this man she trusted.

'Cheers.' He raised his glass. She raised hers back. They both sipped...and grimaced. 'Sorry,' he murmured. 'There wasn't a whole lot of choice at the hotel.'

'Don't apologise. This is nice.' She gestured to the bottle. 'Makes me feel like a grown-up.'

Which, perhaps, wasn't the message she should be broadcasting. 'I mean it's such a change from sitting holding a toy car or a super-soaker or someone's crayon that—'

'I knew what you meant.'

His words, soft and warm in the dark, skimmed the bare surface of her arms and neck and she had to suppress a shiver. A *sexy* shiver. For heaven's sake, she had to find a way to get over this stupid awareness. She glanced at Aidan. And this stupid awkwardness. She'd been fine before she'd started lusting after him. She'd been fine when they'd been talking about his mother.

Speaking of which...

'Have you spoken to your mother tonight?'

'Yes.'

He didn't elaborate. She bit the inside of her cheek and then took a hasty sip of wine. 'It improves on a second tasting,' she offered.

He suddenly laughed. 'You're minding your manners beautifully. To answer the question you refuse to ask, your little suggestion has worked a treat. My mother is racing into my office first thing tomorrow to make sure everything is ship-shape. And heaven help my staff if it's not.'

'Have you warned them?'

'Oh, yes.'

'And your mother seemed...' Happy was too much to hope for. 'Engaged?'

'Yes,' he murmured. 'Yes, she did.'

'Well, that's good isn't it?' He sounded pleased and not pleased at the same time.

'Of course it's good.'

He didn't add anything else.

Okay. Um...

Quinn went back to staring at the stars until the silence chafed too badly. She risked a glance at her travelling companion and found him staring into his wine glass with pursed lips.

'So...uh...are you staying at the caravan park too?'

'I'm staying in one of the cabins here.'

He didn't say anything else. It took all her will-power to stop from jiggling her legs. Tonight this silence with Aidan was too fraught. She wanted the distraction of conversation. 'So...' She decided against asking if his cabin was nice or not. It might be a step up from a caravan, but she expected it would still be fairly basic. 'Have you always wanted to be a politician?'

'No.' The word shot out of him. A moment later his head snapped up. 'I mean, I know that's what the Fairhalls do and what we're known for, but it was always Daniel's passion, not mine.'

A sliver of ice traced a path down her back. 'What were you doing before you made the move to politics?'

'I was a lawyer.'

'Oh?' She injected every ounce of curiosity and interest that she could into that single syllable.

'I worked for a big firm in Sydney that prided itself on its social conscience.' He named the firm.

'I've heard of them!'

'Yeah.' He grinned crookedly and it flipped her heart right over. 'We made the news a lot. We'd take on high profile cases and charge through the nose so we could afford to subsidise the cases we were really interested in.'

'You guys did great work.'

'We did.' He sobered. 'They still do.'

Without him. And that was the moment she realised what he wasn't saying. 'You're keeping the family tradition alive by giving all of that up and going into politics.'

He glanced up as if he'd heard the censure in her voice. 'I will do good work in politics too, Quinn.'

'I don't doubt it.' But at what cost to himself?

The silence between them stretched. Eventually she cleared her throat. 'You know what you said to me yesterday afternoon about who I reminded you of?'

He stilled.

'Is that a good thing or a bad thing?' Did it bring him pain to spend time in her company?

His lips lifted. It was as if she'd removed a weight from him. He met her gaze. 'A good thing.'

She didn't know what to say after that.

He went to top up her glass but she snatched it up and shook her head. 'I really should go to bed now.'

'It's not even eight o'clock.' He set the wine bottle down with an audible thump. 'What are you afraid of, Quinn? That I'm going to make a pass at you and pressure you to have sex with me?'

The thought filled her with a heat almost impossible to ignore, although she did her best to do precisely that. 'I don't want to give you the wrong impression.'

'You're not.'

She leaned towards him. 'I haven't done anything impulsive in a very long time. To be honest, me and impulsive are barely on speaking terms these days. But this trip, and you, it feels as if...'

'What?'

He'd stilled but she recognised the hunger burning deep in his eyes. 'This trip feels like a time-out from the real world, and it feels as if what happens now couldn't possibly affect the future.'

'And that scares you.'

'You're darn tootin' it scares me. I know it's an illusion, a lie. How on earth do you think I ended up single with two children?'

Even in the dark she could see the way he paled.

'Aidan, we're from two different worlds.' Which wasn't precisely true. 'And we're on two different paths.' Which was. 'You're a politician who certainly doesn't want to blot his copybook by doing something reckless. And I'm a single mum who can't afford the luxury of recklessness.'

She stared down at her hands. 'I've turned my whole world upside down and there's a part of me that's screaming in panic. I like you, you're a very attractive man, but I don't want to go looking for comfort and reassurance where I shouldn't. Experience warns me it will only get me into trouble.'

'I don't want to cause you any trouble, Quinn.'

'I know that.' She rose. 'Which is why I'm going to bed. I'll see you in the morning. Thank you for the wine.'

He didn't say anything, but she could feel the weight of his gaze and it slowed her steps. But it didn't stop them.

CHAPTER FOUR

AIDAN MADE COFFEE—instant—from the complimentary jug and tiny sachets in his cabin. The cheap shorts and T-shirt he'd bought at a discount store in Norseman's surprisingly adequate shopping strip yesterday scraped against his skin with an unfamiliar stiffness. That said, they were strangely comfortable, even if they didn't fit as well as the closetful of designer clothes he had in his apartment in Sydney. He slid on his brand new tennis shoes and, mug in hand, headed outside.

The harsh Outback light bouncing off caravan windows made him blink and he had to squint until his eyes adjusted. He'd slept later than he'd meant to, but with the easy, unhurried hours Quinn kept he didn't think that'd be a problem. He glanced around and something tugged at him, something off-key that he couldn't identify. Stifling a yawn, he shrugged it off. This whole situation was strange and off-key.

He ambled up and down the line of cabins and caravans for a bit, reminding himself to get what exercise he could. Mind you, they were only going as far as Madura today—less than six hours of driving. He spent twice that long in his office chair most days.

For pity's sake, they were still only eight hours from Perth! They had another twenty to go before they reached Adelaide. That was what was off-key—this plodding, leisurely pace. He sipped coffee and then frowned. No, what was off-key was his easy acceptance of it.

He closed his eyes and shadows danced behind his eyelids as he acknowledged his utter disinterest in returning to Sydney and his wretched campaign.

But the way his mother's voice had quickened on the phone last night. He forced his eyes open again. Her immediate interest and concern had pulled her out from beneath a morass of apathy. Just like that.

It was why he'd bought the wine. It was why he'd sought out Quinn's company. He'd been searching for solace and reassurance.

Liar.

He blinked.

You wanted her. You still want her. You hoped—

No he didn't! His head reared back. He...

His brain synapses slowed to the consistency of cold treacle. Realisation spread like a toxic chill. He *did* find Quinn attractive. *Very* attractive. From the moment when he'd nearly kissed her yesterday he hadn't been able to get the thought of what she'd taste like out of his mind.

He scratched a hand through his hair and scowled at his feet. Why had he hidden his motives behind a barricade of petty justifications and oh-woe-is-me excuses?

His lungs suddenly cramped. Because of Danny? Because Danny was no longer around to pursue and woo a pretty woman?

For a moment he thought he might throw up.

And then, out of all the spinning chaos in his mind, one tiny shard of comprehension detached itself. That sense of wrongness when he'd stepped out of his cabin...

He spun, coffee flying out in an arc around him. Her car was gone. Quinn's car was gone. She'd left him. *Abandoned* him!

Air punched out of his lungs. He bent at the waist, resting a hand against his knee, while he fought to get oxygen back into his body. He'd screwed up. *Royally.* Quinn's every instinct last night had been spot on. He might've lied to himself, but she'd seen through him. He'd gone looking for temporary respite in its nearest available form—Quinn.

Why? Because he'd felt backed into a corner after that phone call with his mother? What on earth did that have to do with Quinn? *Nothing*!

He straightened. Taking, that was all he'd been interested in. He deserved this. Totally deserved it. But...

He braced an arm against the side of Quinn's caravan—Quinn's *empty* caravan—and rested his head against it.

'Aidan?'

He lifted his head.

'Aidan?'

He jerked around.

Quinn!

'What's wrong?' Her brows drew together.

He glanced beyond her to see the station wagon parked on the other side of the caravan. Robbie and Chase loitered nearby. 'I, uh...just waking up. Where have you been?' His voice came out on a croak.

'Just into town to grab some supplies. This is

the last decent-sized town now until we reach
Ceduna or Port Augusta.' She shrugged. 'On impulse we popped out to the Beacon Hill lookout.'
She shifted her weight. 'I left a message for you
at reception in case you were looking for us.'

Of course she had!

She frowned then and planted her hands on
her hips. He didn't want her to question him too
closely. 'What time do you want to set off?'

'Within the hour.'

'I'll...um...go get packed up.'

He stumbled back into his cabin and collapsed
onto the sofa and dropped his head to his hands,
his coffee mug still dangling from his fingers.
He'd been given a second chance.

Don't mess it up!

Aidan intended on being the best darn travelling
companion Quinn and her kids had ever had.

With his encouragement, the boys spent most
of the first hour telling him about the Beacon Hill
lookout. They'd seen salt lakes and giant mine
tailing dumps. The view obviously hadn't been
pretty, but it had certainly left an impression.
He tried to squash the sense of having been left
out. Instead he recalled his gratitude when he'd

lifted his head to see Quinn standing in front of him this morning.

The talk moved from that lookout in particular to lookouts in general and Aidan found himself trying to describe the view from Corcovado in Rio de Janeiro.

And to then explaining that there weren't any tigers in South America, other than in zoos. Which in turn led to a discussion about zoos. The boys loved zoos—no surprises there. 'You should get your mum to take you to Taronga Park Zoo in Sydney once you've settled in. It'll only be a couple of hours in the car.'

'You live in Sydney,' Robbie said. 'You could come too.'

'If I'm free it's a date,' he promised.

Quinn glanced at her watch. 'Okay, you have an hour of Gameboy time if you want it.'

The boys were soon immersed in their games. She glanced at him, their eyes clashed for the merest fraction of a second before she whipped her gaze back to the road. Damn it! He didn't want her feeling tense around him. He wanted her relaxed and happy. Not because he wanted to seduce her, but because she was a nice woman who'd helped him out and she deserved good things in return.

He shifted on his seat, cleared his throat. 'I've gotta say the variety and splendour of this scenery is something to behold.'

'Uh-huh. Dirt and scrub for as far as the eye can see. You could go a long way before seeing something so...'

'Appealing? Engaging? Captivating?' All words that could describe her. He cut off further musings in that direction. It wasn't going to happen.

'It's amazing, though, isn't it?' she said. 'It's so unvarying, so...unrelieved.'

'I think it's amazing anyone can eke a living out here.'

She puffed out a breath. 'I don't think I could live so far from civilisation.'

Polite chit-chat. Nothing threatening. He excelled at this stuff. He bit back a sigh.

From the corner of his eye he saw her glance at him again. He lifted his chin. 'Do you know we're now on the single longest piece of straight road in Australia?'

'A hundred and forty-six point six kilometres.' She did know.

'Aidan, you're being great with the boys and

I appreciate it, but I don't want you to feel as if you have to make promises to them.'

The change in topic threw him. 'I don't. I...' He stared at her. 'You mean the zoo?'

She nodded.

He rolled his shoulders and stared back out to the front. 'If you want the truth, I'd love to spend the day with you and the boys at the zoo.'

Her knuckles whitened around the steering wheel and he snatched back a curse. 'I've not had much to do with kids. I didn't know...'

She didn't look at him. 'What?'

'I didn't know how much fun they'd be or how much I'd enjoy their company.'

Her knuckles returned to their normal colour. 'Really?'

'I always figured I'd marry and have kids one day. I mean, it's what you do, isn't it?' He scraped a hand across his jaw. 'But... Now I *know* that's what I want.'

The softest of smiles touched her lips and an ache started up deep inside him. An ache that stretched and burned and settled in his groin. He shifted on the seat and did what he could to ignore it. 'I gotta tell you the conversation I had with the boys over hopscotch yesterday.'

He proceeded to tell her about Robbie's question and the plan they'd concocted between them, embellishing where he could until she was laughing so hard he had to reach out and help her steer for a moment.

'Oh, that's priceless.' She dabbed at her eyes—first with her left wrist and then with her right.

She had colour in her cheeks. She'd stopped biting her lip every other minute. He settled back into his seat and listened as she hummed along to a song on the radio. The view outside hadn't changed—still an unending expanse of sand and scrub—but it somehow looked brighter and more inviting than it had earlier.

They reached Madura late afternoon. They'd had what Chase quaintly phrased 'pit stops' at Balladonia and Caiguna. Settlements that were mere specks on the maps. Balladonia had a population of nine. Nine! That put the concept of isolation into perspective. The boys had a lot of fun choosing the nine people they'd most like to have in town...and the nine they'd least want.

Like the rest of the Nullarbor Plain, they were dry dusty places with that same endless low scrub. But they did have roadhouses and accommodation.

Madura was a little larger and some would say a little more scenic, situated as it was at the base of the Hampton Tablelands. As far as Aidan could tell, that just meant that the land undulated a bit more. They booked rooms at the motel and the boys were over the moon to discover it had a pool.

Which was how Aidan found himself wandering around outside the pool fence with Quinn while the boys splashed and whooped inside. Out of the corner of his eye he saw Robbie race from one end of the pool enclosure to the other as a run-up for a big jump into the water. It had been a long time since he could remember running for the sheer joy of it. He wouldn't mind running now.

He ran a finger around the collar of his T-shirt and reminded himself he was a grown man. 'Quinn, about last night...'

She tensed. She tensed so much she stopped walking.

He squinted at the sky. 'Last night I was feeling at a bit of a loss. I didn't know what to do with myself.'

She started a jerky forward motion again. 'Because of your conversation with your mother?'

'Do you think it's crazy of me to worry about her?'

'No.'

His collar stopped trying to strangle him.

She glanced at him. 'Do you read?'

'Sure I do. Not that I get much time for it.' When she raised an exaggerated eyebrow he had to nod. 'You're right, there's plenty of time for it at the moment.'

'If you're interested, I have a few books in the back of the car.'

Reading for pleasure had become a rare treat. He straightened. 'I'd love to borrow one.'

'C'mon, then.' She hitched her head in the direction of the car.

She moved with the grace of a gazelle, dainty and elegant, though neither of those things hid her supple strength. He had to force his gaze from the long length of her legs and back to his surroundings before he betrayed himself.

She shifted a couple of boxes in the wagon and then pointed. 'That box there, can you drag it out?'

He did. When he peered inside it his lip started to curl. 'Science textbooks?'

Her grin was sudden and swift and he thanked heaven he was leaning against the car or he might've fallen face first into the dirt. 'I worked in one of the science departments at the University of Western Australia and one of the professors had a clean-out of his bookshelves last week. I helped myself to a couple.'

Good Lord, why? He didn't ask, but she must've seen the question in his face. 'If you find such things dull and dry, they're guaranteed to put you to sleep in five minutes flat.'

She didn't find them dull or dry, though, did she? What had she meant to do with her life before fate had intervened in the shape of an unplanned pregnancy? He stared at the textbooks.

'Dig deeper.' She nodded at the box. 'There's quite a selection in there.'

He chose an autobiography of a famous actor. He turned it face out to show her. 'Do you mind? I've been wanting to read this for ages.'

'Help yourself.'

He packed the box back up and stacked it in its original position. When he finished he turned to find her leaning against the car with her eyes closed and her face lifted to the sun.

A breath eased out of him.

Her eyes sprang open. 'What?'

Stop staring! He shut the trunk. 'I was just thinking how much more relaxed you look today than you did yesterday or the day before.'

'Oh, that.' She blinked and then she smiled and it was such a beautiful smile the breath punched out of him all over again. There were moments when this woman smiled with her whole being, the way Daniel used to. It made him crave something he had no name for.

'When we set off from Perth I started having panic attacks wondering if I was doing the right thing or not.'

'And now?' His heart pounded though he couldn't have explained why.

'Now I've decided to embrace what's ahead of me—to enjoy it and make the absolute best of it.'

'Bravo!' No sooner had the word left his mouth than his mind started to whirl. Could he take a leaf out of her book, follow her example? Could he find a way to embrace the course set before his feet—the political life?

His legs and shoulders grew heavy. The day

darkened, even though the sun remained high and warm above them.

They started walking again because their only two options were walking or sitting and they'd both had enough of sitting.

He supposed he could excuse himself and retire to his room with the book. He didn't want to, though. There'd be enough time for solitude later. He rolled his shoulders and tried to throw off his funk. 'What are you hoping to gain from your move, Quinn?' Considering her future—and the boys'—was a more promising option than trying to make sense of his. Still, he intended to retract the question if it made her look the least bit uncomfortable.

A breath eased out of him when it didn't.

She nodded towards the boys and he had to remind himself not to hold her gaze for too long. *Don't let her see how much you want to kiss her.*

He watched the two boys dive simultaneously into the pool. He clapped his hands and shouted praise.

He glanced from them and back to their mother. Steel flooded his spine. He was not going to mess with her. Him and her, they were on different courses and he had no intention of dragging her or her boys into his own private hell.

What are you hoping to gain from your move?

Aidan's words scored through her. Quinn twisted her hands together and watched her boys. They were so absorbed in their splashing and diving, and her heart filled with so much love it almost hurt.

She pointed a finger at Chase, who looked as if he was about to tear off down the other end of the enclosure. 'No running,' she said for the second time. 'Wet feet and wet concrete are not a good combination.' Her second son had a tendency to learn his lessons the hard way.

She glanced back to find Aidan watching her with a queer light in his eyes. She didn't know what it meant. Today he'd been so *friendly* that she'd started to think she'd been mistaken about the vibes she'd sensed last night.

He might not want you, but you still want him.

He must know lots of beautiful polished women. The idea of him being attracted to a single mother who wore next to no make-up and didn't give two hoots about designer outfits was laughable.

She tried to push that thought aside, tried to shake off the heaviness that threatened to descend and to concentrate on what really was important—her move across the country.

What are you hoping to gain from your move?

'Family,' she finally said. 'I'm hoping to give my boys, my aunt and myself a family.'

'Family,' he repeated, annunciating each syllable in a kind of slow homage to the word.

'You're close to your parents.' She wasn't sure if she was asking or stating.

'I guess.'

But he'd become guarded, wary, and her heart burned for him. She refused to pry, though. He and his parents had suffered so much. She dredged up a smile and a shrug. 'I found myself watching my friends in Perth over the last year and seeing what a source of strength their families were to them. I'm talking about extended families—parents, grandparents, siblings, cousins, aunts and uncles—and I started to envy them.'

Somewhere along the line she'd stopped walking. She kicked herself back into action, forced one foot in front of the other. Aidan's long legs kept easy pace beside her. The sun had started to lower in the west and the scrub, low trees and sand all glowed orange and khaki. A sigh eased out of her. 'I know their families were occasionally—even often—a source of frustration, but they were a source of happiness too.' A source of belonging.

'And you want that?'

'Yes.' With all her heart and she wasn't ashamed to admit it. She knew her own strength. She knew she could continue to go it alone. But if she didn't have to…

'And as I only have one relation who is the slightest bit interested in wanting to know me…' She'd made her voice tongue-in-cheek, but Aidan didn't smile.

She reached out and pulled him to a halt. His arm flexed beneath her fingers and she sensed its latent strength. Reluctantly she released him. 'I'm tired of feeling alone, Aidan.'

She didn't know what it was about this man that made her so ready to confide in him. Maybe it was the innate 'ships passing in the night' nature of their association. It had broken down the usual barriers of reserve.

His face became gentle. He reached out as if to touch her cheek, but he drew his hand back at the last moment. The usual barriers hadn't broken down that much.

'Don't get me wrong.' She forced herself to start walking again. 'I'm not lonely. I have friends, colleagues, not to mention my boys. I'm not unhappy. It's just when I have to make a decision about one of the boys—should I go up to the school and make an issue about Chase's appalling handwriting or another child's constant use of a bad word, or should I let Robbie stay up late on the occasional Saturday night so he can watch a rugby test match, or any number of things like that. To be able to talk it over with someone who's also invested would be such a comfort. Even if we didn't agree.'

'Wow,' he eventually breathed.

She immediately cringed. 'Sorry, that was probably way more information than you wanted and—'

'Mum!'

Chase's scream and Robbie's shout had her spinning around, adrenaline flooding her every cell. Heart pounding, she raced for the gate, all instinct and fear.

Blood.

Blood in the water.

Chase in the water.

She tugged and tugged on the safety latch on the gate, but her fingers kept slipping and finding no purchase, as if she'd forgotten how to use an opposable thumb. Her breath came hard and short in little sobs. *Please, gate. Please open.*

It wouldn't open!

In one easy vault, Aidan cleared the fence and, without breaking stride, dived into the water and pulled Chase into his arms. 'He's okay,' he called to her.

Okay meant he wasn't drowned. It didn't mean he was *okay.*

Magically the gate opened and she flew to Aidan as he emerged with a howling Chase from the shallow end. There was so much blood!

She reached for him and Chase reached for her, but Aidan pushed her down onto the banana lounge that held the boys' towels and shirts before setting Chase onto her lap.

She held him close and rocked him, murmuring nonsense in an effort to quiet him, while Aidan tried to stem the blood from the cut above Chase's eye. She handed him one of the shirts she half sat on. They could replace a shirt, but she would never be able to replace one of her beautiful boys.

Her heart thunderstormed in her chest as she watched Aidan's face, trying to gauge the extent of the damage by his expression, but he kept his face carefully schooled and she couldn't read it at all.

Fear gripped her by the throat. If Chase were badly hurt...way out here in the back of beyond, it'd be her fault.

Please God. Please God. Please God.

She glanced up to find Robbie staring at her with fear in his eyes. She did what she could to swallow her own. 'What happened, honey?'

Robbie scuffed a toe against the cement. 'He, um...slipped and hit his head on the side of the pool before falling in.'

They'd been running! She should've been keeping a closer eye on them! She should've been watching them properly, not pouring her heart out to the first man who'd shown a modicum of interest in her in months!

Aidan straightened and her gaze flew back to him. 'What?' She couldn't push anything else out.

'He's going to have a heck of a lump and a shiner tomorrow, and probably a corker of a headache tonight, but the cut's not deep and it won't need stitches.'

She closed her eyes and sent up a prayer of thanks. 'There was so much blood,' she whispered.

'Head wounds bleed a lot.' He sat back on his heels, a smile touching his lips. 'With two young sons, I'd have thought you'd have known that.'

Crazily, she found herself almost smiling back.

Chase's sobs had eased and Aidan gestured to him. 'I'd like to check him for concussion.'

'Hey, baby,' she crooned. 'Can you look at Mummy?'

Chase sat up a bit and touched his head. 'It hurts,' he hiccupped.

'I bet it does. That was a heck of a tumble,' she soothed, smoothing his hair back.

'There was blood.' His lip wobbled.

'You're not wrong about that, buddy.' Aidan crouched down in front of them. 'We're going to play a quick game.' He hurried on before Chase could refuse and bury his head in her shoulder again. 'How many fingers am I holding up?'

'Three.'

'What's my name?'

'Aidan.'

'And what comes after D in the alphabet?'

Chase started reciting the alphabet under his breath. 'E.'

'Excellent, Chase, you got a perfect score.'

Chase snuggled into her and started to shiver. Aidan grabbed a towel and wrapped it around the child. 'We need to get him warm and dry.'

'How do you know so much about this?' Aidan seemed so calm and professional—utterly unfazed, unlike her. Besides, talking kept the demons at bay.

'I did a St John's Ambulance course six months ago.'

She struggled to her feet. In another year Chase would be too big for her to carry. But she could still manage it at the moment. 'What made you decide to do that? Not that I'm not grateful, of course, but—'

She broke off. Daniel. The car accident.

Right.

In his grief, Aidan had chosen to do something positive rather than negative. Good for him.

'Thank you,' she murmured when he opened the gate for her.

'You're welcome.'

And then he draped a towel around the shoulders of a too quiet Robbie and rested his arm across her eldest son's shoulders in a gesture of comfort and companionship and walked them back to their room.

It didn't make her knees weak. It didn't make her pulse quicken. But it did make her heart tremble.

Aidan was sitting to one side of her door in a camp chair when she slipped out of her room that night. He rose and set another chair out for her.

And then he handed her a can of beer.

And a chocolate bar.

Tears pricked her eyes. A big lump lodged in her throat, making it impossible to squeeze out so much as a thank you. She sat.

'Thought you could do with a pick-me-up.'

She nodded, sniffled and pulled in a breath that made her entire frame shudder. And then she opened her beer and took a gulp. She tore open the wrapper of her chocolate bar and took a big bite.

She closed her eyes, sat back and let the tension drain out of her. She drank more beer. She ate more chocolate. It was a disgusting combination and she relished every single mouthful.

Aidan sat with his legs stretched out and eyes to the front, quietly surveying the night. No rush or impatience or expectation. His stillness slowly eased into her. She finished both the beer and the chocolate bar. 'That's exactly what I needed.'

'Good.'

'Thank you.'

'You're welcome.'

She turned to him as much as her tired limbs would allow. 'I want to thank you for springing into action so quickly today.'

'It was no big deal.'

'It was a huge deal to me. I couldn't even get the rotten gate open.'

'You would've eventually.'

She shuddered. 'Chase could've drowned by then.'

'Stop exaggerating,' he chided. 'He was holding his head out of the water when I got to him.'

He had been? A little more of the residual fear eased out of her.

'He was just a bit dazed and in pain. How is he now?'

'Asleep, thankfully. They were both exhausted.'

'And how are you?'

She sent him a wan smile. 'Well, I've slowed

down on the blame game and I'm slowly recovering from the fright.' She stared out towards the scrub beyond the circle of light cast from the motel, but she couldn't see a thing. It was all deep blackness. 'I never knew I could feel so afraid until I had children.'

'Did I really say earlier that I wanted them?'

She laughed. 'It's worth it.' But not if you worked in excess of eighty hours a week. She glanced at him. She opened her mouth. She closed it again. *None of your business.*

They were both silent for a while. 'Funny, isn't it?' she eventually said. 'How love and pain can be so closely linked. Not just romantic love, but love for one's children and parents and friends.'

Though this man knew more about that than most. 'Still—' she pulled in a breath '—life's not worth living without it.'

'Which makes the human race either incredibly stupid or incredibly brave.'

'I'll go with brave if they're the only two options on offer.'

She was rewarded with a lopsided grin and a shake of his head.

'I thought you were very brave today. I'm in

your debt, Aidan. I doubt I'll ever be able to repay you, but if there's anything I can do...ever...'

He turned to her and behind the tempting brightness of his eyes she sensed his mind racing. 'There might be one thing you could do...'

The look on his face made her breath catch and her stomach do slow loop the loops.

He wouldn't!

He rose. 'I'll give it some thought and let you know in the morning. Goodnight, Quinn.'

She could only stare after him, wondering what on earth he was playing at. Or if he was playing at anything at all.

CHAPTER FIVE

THE NEXT MORNING Quinn and the boys enjoyed a picnic breakfast at a table near the pool. It wasn't fancy—cereal and toast. Quinn had lugged cereal and long-life milk with her from Perth. She'd bought fresh bread from the roadhouse that morning.

While it might not be fancy, the warm morning and the novelty filled the boys with glee and took their minds off eating in the roadhouse restaurant. It wasn't that she needed to count every penny, but she did want to be careful. Besides, she wanted them to eat as healthily as she could manage whilst on the road.

She was blowing on her coffee when Aidan sauntered into view. The steam floated up into her face, haloing him in a smoky soft focus. He looked like a mirage, like a man walking out of the desert. A sigh breathed out of her and more steam drifted upwards.

She shook herself and then blew on her coffee

until the steam blinded her. When he reached the table, she smiled in his direction, but took a moment to hand Robbie a paper napkin so she didn't have to address him. Of course, that didn't block his scent when he sat beside her. She breathed him in, and the knot in her chest unwound.

'Morning, troops.'

The boys sing-songed their greetings back to him through mouthfuls of Vegemite toast.

'Have you eaten?' She sort of half glanced at him. His hair was damp as if he'd just showered and he wore a different T-shirt than he had yesterday. The T-shirt had obviously come in a packet and two creases bisected his chest and another his stomach. He looked utterly different from the man who'd begged her for a ride. Her father wouldn't have approved. She did, wholeheartedly.

'Help yourself.' She gestured to the cereal boxes and pile of toast. 'There's another cereal bowl in our room if you'd like it.'

He nodded behind him to the roadhouse. 'I've already eaten.'

She hoped his breakfast had been healthy. She opened her mouth. She closed it again. *None of your business.*

He glanced at their table. 'But this looks nice.'

She couldn't mistake his wistfulness, though it was harder to explain the burn in her heart. 'Well, you're absolutely welcome to join us for soggy cereal and cold toast tomorrow.'

He laughed as she'd meant him to, but the burn in her heart only intensified.

He glanced at Chase. 'How's the head, buster?'

'It's better.' He glowered at Quinn. 'I keep telling Mum I'm all better and that I can go swimming in the pool again, but she won't listen.'

She had to bite back a smile. Both of her children would need to be seriously under the weather to resist the lure of a swim.

'Your mum is probably right. A quiet day could be just the thing.'

Chase heaved a sigh, evidently exasperated with clueless adults.

'Which is why I want to run a proposal by you all.'

Aidan ran a hand down his shirt as if to smooth out the creases and she suddenly realised she'd been staring. She shook herself. 'Proposal?'

His look told her he was thinking of last night and her 'returning the favour' remark. The boys glanced to her and she sat up a little straighter. 'We're all ears.'

'I was thinking we could all do with a day off from driving.'

She'd been working on the theory that it'd take them ten days to reach Aunt Mara's, longer if they decided to tarry somewhere. With the NSW school holidays currently operating, the boys weren't missing any school. This was only day four of their great 'across the country' expedition, so they weren't even halfway through their journey yet, but she didn't say anything. She was too curious to see what Aidan meant to propose.

In the morning sunshine his eyes twinkled. It could've been the reflection cast up from the pool, but she didn't think so. She had a feeling it came from within. She hadn't seen him fired up with enthusiasm before, except for that moment when he'd talked about his law firm. Now, though, he smiled and twinkled and she could barely drag her gaze away. An answering enthusiasm built through her. 'A day off?'

He leaned in towards her, his smile growing and she pulled in a great breath of him. 'I know you don't want to drive longer than five hours a day if you can help it...'

They'd had to drive five and a half yesterday. It made the boys restless. And look at what had happened at the pool afterwards.

'But if we drove to Penong today—'

'How long?'

'A bit over six hours.'

She grimaced and gestured for him to continue. 'The thing is, Penong is close to a place called Cactus Beach.'

'A beach!' Robbie and Chase gazed at her as if pleading for her to accept any proposal that included a beach.

'Cactus Beach is well known in surfing circles.' Aidan was a surfer? Really?

'If we drive to Penong today, we could spend all of tomorrow at the beach.'

'So…we'd spend two nights at Penong before heading for Port Augusta?'

'That's right.'

The lure of not having to pack up everything for a whole day spoke to her. Loudly.

The boys started shouting out their excited endorsements of Aidan's plan, interspersed with lots of pleading and assurances that Chase was better and that they'd be extra good.

A whole day at the beach? It sounded wonderful. This was exactly the kind of adventure she'd hoped for on their journey. Her boys' excited faces almost sealed the deal, but she forced herself to pull back. It was harder than it should've been. 'What about your burning need to get to Adelaide asap?'

Robbie scowled at Aidan. 'Why you wanna do that? Aren't you having fun with us?'

'I'm having the best time,' Aidan assured him. 'And I have another song to teach you later.'

Robbie's scowl vanished.

Aidan ran his hand down the crease in his T-shirt again. She tried not to follow his hand's progress. 'I think my absence in the office for another couple of days could be a...' The happy light in his eyes faded a little. 'A good thing.'

Why should that leach the happiness from him?

She glanced down at her toast. She'd had a thought or two on that head, but... *It's none of your business*. Then she recalled the way he'd vaulted the pool fence and the way he'd lifted Chase into his arms.

She could make it her business.

At the beach.

'It sounds like the best idea ever.' She crossed her fingers. Aidan grinned. The boys cheered.

She turned to Robbie and Chase. 'It does mean a long time in the car today.'

'We promise to be good.' Robbie nudged Chase, who nodded enthusiastically. 'If we get grumpy we'll just think of the beach and we'll be happy again. It'll make it all worth it.'

Oh, how she wished she could've given them more fun, more outings and holidays in their short lives. She swallowed a lump. 'Okay, then. Let's get this mess cleaned up and start packing.'

They reached Cactus Beach at the end of a long dirt road. The landscape surrounding them amazed Quinn. Nullarbor translated from the Latin to mean no trees and today it definitely lived up to its reputation. Rocks, low scrub and amazing sand dunes stretched out on all sides. When the beach came into view, nobody uttered a word.

A crescent of white sand with rocky outcrops at either end and a sea of jewelled blues and greens spread out before them like an ancient Mecca. It was utterly deserted. And it was utterly beautiful.

The boys just stared at it with their mouths agape. Aidan folded his arms and grinned. She let out a long, low, pent-up breath.

Aidan swung to them, his grin widening. 'Cactus Beach has three perfect surfing breaks—Castles and Cactus which are both left-handers and Caves which is a powerful right hand break.'

'And that's good?'

'It's epic!'

Right. 'I hate to rain on your parade, but you, uh, don't have a surfboard with you.'

He shook his head. 'Doesn't matter. I can now say I've been here.'

Robbie and Chase broke free from their enthralment long enough to tug at her, their excitement palpable. 'Can we, Mum? Huh, can we?'

She'd already slathered them both in sunblock back at their on-site van in Penong. It might be late March, but the sun shone with all of its usual enthusiasm and the faint breeze was warm with the memory of summer. 'Okay, give me your shirts and off you go.'

Both boys raced straight for the water.

She could tell Aidan itched to hit the waves as much as her children did. Still, he waited for her to choose the perfect patch of sand before setting down the cooler bag that practically burst with their supplies for the day. She'd packed sodas, water, sandwiches and fruit. She'd even splurged on cheese and crackers.

'Go on.' She gave him a playful push. 'I can tell you're as eager to be out there as Robbie and Chase.'

She glanced at the boys. For all of his talk of big breaks, the surf was remarkably gentle today.

He flashed a grin that made her heart stutter before dragging his shirt over his head and revealing a perfectly toned torso. Wind instantly rushed in her ears, filling her head with noise. She stared, pressing hands to cheeks that had grown red-hot. With a start she pulled them away and pushed them into the small of her back instead and pretended to stretch, praying he hadn't noticed her heat and confusion…her desire.

She sent up a prayer of thanks when she finally managed to make her eyes focus. He just stood there as if relishing the feel of the sun against his bare skin. She glanced away, having to fight the urge to reach out and touch him. For all his talk of castles and caves and whatnot, he wasn't what she'd call tanned for this time of year. Exactly how many hours was he putting in at that office of his?

Her lips twisted. At the moment she'd bet eighty-hour weeks were a conservative guess. The thought made her shudder. It eased the burn threatening to consume her too. He might have a hot body—the hottest she'd seen in a very long time—and he might be a nice man—the nicest she'd come across in a very long time—but his lifestyle was repugnant to her. Why would someone embark on a relationship with a man like him? You'd never see him long enough to enjoy the hot body or to indulge in long, intimate conversations.

Why? Her lips twisted. Status, standing and prestige, not to mention wealth. That was why. And none of that could tempt her.

He took a step towards the water. 'I hope you're wearing sunscreen.' As soon as the words left her mouth, she realised how ludicrous they were. The man had been trying to get a flight out of Perth. One thing he hadn't been doing was planning a beach holiday.

He turned back and his grin when it came was low and wicked. She wanted to respond. She wanted to take the bottle of lotion from her bag, amble over to him with a sinuous swing of her hips and slowly rub lotion into his shoulders, his back and his chest. She'd like to—

She snapped herself out of her fantasy—

reminded herself about eighty-hour working weeks—seized the bottle of sunscreen and tossed it to him.

'Are you coming in?' he asked when he was done, handing the bottle back to her.

He hadn't been able to reach all of his back. *Not your problem.*

With a sigh she took the bottle from him and poured lotion into her hand. She didn't need a travelling companion with a serious case of sunburn. Or sunstroke. She slathered it on his back with as much cool efficiency as she could muster. Reciting the periodic table in her mind helped.

'Would you like me to return the favour?'

She recapped the bottle a little too vigorously. 'Uh, no thank you. Robbie and Chase took care of it earlier.'

'So, are you coming in?'

That was when she realised she'd been biting her lip the entire time. She released it. 'Sure I am. In a bit.' She couldn't explain why, but she didn't want to pull her sundress over her head to stand in front of him in nothing but her birthday suit.

Bathing suit! Lord, talk about a Freudian slip.

She was a mother. She had responsibilities. Ignoring Aidan, she walked down to the shore to paddle and keep an eye on the boys. She was no longer that impulsive girl who'd let passion rule her head. Even if a remnant of that girl remained in the woman she'd become.

Eventually, though, the lure of the water became too much and she tossed her dress to the sand. She splashed with the boys. She laughed and relaxed and forgot to worry about anything for a while.

Chase didn't have Robbie's confidence in the surf, but he begged her to take him out to the deeper water. Robbie wanted to go out too. He was a good swimmer, but if either one of them got into trouble she'd be hard pressed to deal with the both of them. She was about to suggest she take them out one at a time, but suddenly Aidan was there with a summer grin and holiday eyes.

'Hey, Robbie, you wanna learn how to body surf?'

'Yes!'

So they all moved into the deeper water beyond the break of the waves. The gentle rolling of the swell rocked them and it eased the frenetic craziness of the last few weeks. She gave Chase a swimming lesson, and then they both floated for a while. She turned her head to watch Aidan and Robbie.

A laugh spurted out of her oldest son and then he looked up at Aidan as if...

She straightened. Her heart caught and then vibrated with sudden pain. Aidan was all kindness and attention and her eldest son was blossoming under that influence. In fact, Robbie lapped up every scrap of Aidan's attention like a starving dog.

Her eyes stung. She knew he hungered for this kind of male bonding. If only Phillip would spend more time with his sons!

'Ow, Mum, you're hurting my hand!'

She immediately relaxed her grip on Chase's hand. 'Sorry, honey.'

'Can we go in so I can jump over the waves again?'

'Sure we can.'

She and Chase jumped waves, but the entire time she could see her eldest son's hero worship growing—it was reflected in the way he laughed too loudly, the way he gazed up at Aidan, and in his absolute lack of self-consciousness as he came out of his usual reserved shell.

Damn it! Why couldn't she be everything her

sons needed? Why couldn't she be both mother and father to them? She didn't want them to lack for anything and it wasn't right that they should.

She re-tied her ponytail. She only had one set of arms and one set of legs, though, and there were two of them and some days she was spread too thin as it was.

'Are you okay?'

She jumped to find Aidan beside her, staring down at her with narrowed eyes. She spun and located both Robbie and Chase. 'Yes, I'm perfect.'

'I'll second that.' He grinned down at her and it snapped her out of her funk in an instant. The remnant of the reckless girl she'd once been gave a long, low stretch. Her common sense raised an eyebrow. She had to bite back a groan. If she weren't careful she'd end up with a serious case of hero worship too.

Robbie insisted on sitting next to Aidan when they had lunch. He argued about putting his shirt and hat back on, until Aidan put his shirt on too.

She liked Aidan. She liked him a lot, but it would do Robbie no good to become too attached to him. They'd see neither hide nor hair of Aidan once this adventure was over.

Aidan would return to his relentless workload and his social position and his prominence on the political landscape and he'd have no time for surfing with young boys.

She rested back on one hand and bit into an apple. 'I guess we'd best make the most of your company while we have it, Aidan. I mean in another two days we'll be in Adelaide.'

Robbie stared from Aidan to her. 'What happens in Adelaide?'

'The plane strike ended today so I guess Aidan will catch a plane back to Sydney.'

'But we could drop him off in Sydney in the car.'

'We could,' she agreed. It took an effort to keep the smile on her face and her voice breezy. 'But it'll take a few days longer and Aidan can't afford any more time off work.'

Aidan looked as if she'd slapped him. *Oh, Aidan...* She ached to reach out and hug him.

'Aidan could come visit us at Aunt Mara's.'

''Course he can,' she agreed. 'Just as soon as he has some free time.'

Robbie's face fell and she knew he was thinking of his father's endless litany of excuses for why he couldn't visit. *Oh, Robbie...* She wanted to hug him and never let him go. But that wouldn't help him either, not in the long term.

'Hey, who wants to go and explore the rock pools over there?'

That distracted both of the boys. She packed up the remnants of their lunch before grabbing the can of soda she hadn't finished yet. The boys raced ahead.

'Are you looking forward to getting rid of me?'

The bluntness of Aidan's question shattered her carefully constructed veneer. 'Oh, Aidan, no.' She reached out to grip his arm. 'I don't know if you realise this or not, but Robbie is developing a serious case of hero worship where you're concerned.'

'I…' He blinked.

'You're being great with him. I don't want you to change the way you are…'

'But?'

She realised she still held him. She let him go. 'These aren't waters I've had to navigate before.' Adelaide loomed ahead like a dark cloud. 'I just want him to be prepared for when we do part company, that's all. I wasn't trying to make you feel unwanted.'

He grimaced and scratched a hand through his hair. 'Sorry, I'm not usually so touchy.'

But they'd been having the most perfect day and her words had obviously taken him off guard.

'I'm clueless—' he waved towards Robbie '—about the whole kid thing.'

'So am I some days.'

'What about their father? Where's he?'

'In London at the moment. When he's in Australia he's mostly in Sydney. His contact with the boys is erratic.' It was the politest way she could put it.

Aidan called Phillip such a rude name she snorted soda out of her nose. Not that she disagreed with him. 'That's one way of putting it.'

'Sorry.'

'You are not.' But she didn't mind in the least. 'He claims that our living in Perth makes it difficult for him to visit. But now surely a two-hour drive north isn't too much of an effort when he is in the country. I'm hoping this move means Phillip will start spending more time with Robbie and Chase. God knows they crave it.'

He stopped and fixed her with those fiery amber eyes. 'That's the real reason you're moving, isn't it?'

He said it as if it were the most amazing thing. She wrinkled her nose and rolled her shoulders.

'It is, isn't it?'

It was part of it. So what? 'There are a whole host of reasons.'

He caught her hand, pulled her to a halt, turning her to face him. 'It is, isn't it?'

The warmth and sympathy in his eyes had a lump wedging in her throat. She wanted to fling herself into his arms and soak up some of his strength and goodness. But that way lay ruin, as her mother would so quaintly put it.

Instead she very gently disengaged her hand from his. She swallowed. When she was sure her voice would emerge normally she said, 'You know what I hate? That a vast section of our society still looks down on single mothers, thinking they're only out for what they can get. Phillip pays child support, yes. When he first left a part of me wanted no contact and no links, but that's not my decision to make. I have no right putting my pride before my children's welfare.'

Shading her eyes, she turned to survey the boys, who were both clambering over the rocks, safe and occupied. She swung back. 'Another woman once told me she thought it a form of child abuse for a woman to refuse child support from her child's father. She said it'd be depriving the child of a better financial future. And she's right.'

'And now you feel you owe Phillip?'

'No! I owe Robbie and Chase. I owe them a good future. It's my responsibility to ensure they have all the things they need.' And at the moment they ached for their father. At least, Robbie did, and in a couple of years so would Chase.

'But it seems to me that society doesn't commend women for making those kinds of sacrifices. And it seems to me that in the vast majority of cases it's women who do actually make the real sacrifices.'

He stared down at her, his eyes soft. Aidan would never abandon a child. She didn't know what made her so sure, only that she was.

'I think you're amazing. I think you're wonderful.'

She had no hope of hiding how much his words touched her. 'Thank you.'

'I—'

'No,' she warned, keeping her voice crisp. 'Don't lay the compliments on too thick or you'll spoil the effect.'

He laughed. It was a good sound.

'C'mon, let's see what the boys are up to.'

They'd walked five steps when he asked, 'What happened between you and Phillip?'

A sidelong glance told her he wasn't looking at her. In fact he was looking suspiciously nonchalant. Her pulse leapt. She tried to stamp on it. 'That's a story for another day when the boys are in bed.' And while she didn't mean them to, the words emerged as a pledge.

The rest of the day lived up to its perfect promise. They explored the beach. There was more swimming and eating. The boys built sandcastles and as the tide came in the surf built up into the perfect breaks that Aidan had spoken about earlier.

His eyes lit up. 'I'm going to come back here one day with a surfboard.'

The afternoon waned and the sun had started to sink into the sea to the west when she and Aidan drove two very tired boys back to Penong.

After showers and a makeshift dinner of beans on toast, Aidan built a campfire in the pit in front of their on-site vans—he'd chosen to hire the one beside hers rather than stay at the motel—and then produced a bag of marshmallows.

They sat around the fire and toasted marsh-mallows as if they were a real family. Her heart wanted to spring free to dance and twirl but she wouldn't let it.

'It's been the best day in the world,' Chase said, leaning against her.

'The very best,' Robbie said, leaning into her other side.

They both grew heavy with sleep. 'Bedtime, I think,' she murmured to Aidan.

Without asking, without even apparently think-ing about it, he rose and lifted Robbie into his arms, waited until she'd lifted Chase into hers, before following her into the van and helping her put them to bed. Both boys were asleep before she and Aidan left the caravan.

It made the task so much easier with someone to help. If only… She shook her head. She shook her whole body. 'Soda?'

'I bought a bottle of wine.' He rubbed the back of his neck. 'I thought…'

He looked delightfully nonplussed. She shifted from one foot to the other and then finally nod-ded. 'A glass of wine would be lovely.'

They sat beside the dying embers of the fire and sipped wine, staring up into the majesty of a glittering sky. She knew he was still curious about her and her history, but he'd be too polite to ask again. Well, she had questions of her own, and if she talked first maybe he'd open up to her too.

She crossed her fingers.

'I discovered I was pregnant in the time between graduating high school and the start of the university academic year.' Though he didn't move, she sensed she had his full attention. 'To say it was a shock is an understatement. For everyone.'

'You didn't consider an abortion?'

'Sure I did. I was only eighteen. I was supposed to have my whole life in front of me. I had plans. Plans a baby would interfere with.'

'But?'

With his non-judgemental attitude, Aidan would make a very good politician. She wondered if he realised that. 'But my parents and Phillip's parents insisted I have an abortion.'

'And that got your back up?'

'Oh, yes. I sometimes wonder if I only went ahead with the pregnancy just to spite them.' She glanced at him. 'That's not a very edifying thought, is it?'

'And not something I believe for a minute.'

She smiled at the fire. Maybe not. There'd been a part of her that had started loving the child inside her the minute she'd found out she was carrying it. A part of her she hadn't been able to ignore.

'Did Phillip want you to have an abortion too?'

She sipped her wine and then leaned back on one hand. 'Actually, he was really good. He didn't pressure me at all. He was a reasonable human being back then.' She had hopes he'd become one again. 'He said he'd stick by me whatever my decision. I didn't find out for another three years that he'd hoped I'd choose the abortion.' That had been the same night he'd accused her of ruining his life.

'As I believe I mentioned before, my parents cut me off completely when I refused to obey their ultimatum. They thought it'd bring me to heel, but it didn't. Phillip's parents weren't quite so harsh, but they counselled him to go to university as planned and to have minimal contact with me and the baby.'

'Nice.'

His sarcasm wrung a smile from her. 'They

didn't cut him off, but they refused to acknowledge me and I wasn't welcome in their home.'

She crossed her legs. 'So we moved to Perth. He got a job in a bank as a teller. I did a short office admin course and picked up some temp work until the baby came. Robbie was three months old when I picked up some part-time work as an administrative assistant at the university and we put him into childcare two days a week.'

'It sounds tough.'

'Thousands of people do it every year.' She shot him a smile. 'It was a challenge to make ends meet, but we were young and... I loved him.'

Aidan didn't say anything. She glanced at him. 'Have you been in love?'

He shook his head.

'It's wonderful. It gives you wings. It gives you hope. And it can make you very determined. It makes the tough times worthwhile.' She sipped her wine—a cool, crisp Sauvignon Blanc that slipped down her throat smoothly. 'But when love goes bad it's terrible.'

'I'm sorry it went bad for you, Quinn.'

He earned a big fat Brownie point for not asking why it had gone bad. Her fingers tightened about her glass. If she shared that with him, though, maybe he would share with her. She could only try. 'Things were going fine until I fell pregnant with Chase. It sounds dreadfully irresponsible, doesn't it, but we'd used birth control both times I fell pregnant. I'm obviously disgustingly fertile.'

A low rumble left Aidan's throat. It eased the heaviness that threatened to settle over her.

'It was too soon for us to have another child.' And yet she'd felt the same love for it as she had for Robbie.

'Much too soon for us to have another baby,' she whispered again, almost to herself.

'What happened?'

'Phillip panicked.' She shrugged. 'He panicked throughout my pregnancy about how we'd make ends meet. He asked me to have an abortion. I refused. I wanted Robbie to have what I'd never had—a sibling.' A friend. 'Phillip kept right on panicking after Chase was born and he never connected with him the way he had with Robbie. I cut back on our expenses as much as I could, but...'

The fire blurred for a moment. Aidan reached over and took her hand. And bless him. He just waited. He didn't try to hurry her.

'I discovered his secret bank account. He told

me it was his university fund. He hadn't been panicking about how we'd make ends meet at all. He was panicking that he might have to dip into his university fund.'

Air hissed from between Aidan's teeth.

'And then his parents pounced when Phillip was at his weakest.' She pulled her hand from his. 'They offered to pay for him to study in London.'

The night wasn't really silent—there were the chirrups of night birds and insects, and the occasional crackle from the dying embers, but the night pressed in hard around them. Aidan stared at Quinn and ached for her.

'So when Chase was four months old, Phillip left.'

Phillip had left her with two small children? One of them just a baby? The jerk had turned his back on his own flesh and blood? 'The low-life rat scum!'

She gave a small laugh, but the thread of tiredness that stretched through it caught at his heart.

'So there you have it, Aidan, my sordid little story.'

His chin jerked up. 'I don't think it's sordid.'

Not on her part at least. Phillip was another matter. And so were her parents. The people who were supposed to love her had all let her down, abandoned her. He made a vow to himself then to check out her Aunt Mara. He wasn't letting anyone else take advantage of Quinn.

That's not your decision to make.

He ground his teeth together. She was his friend. He'd make it his business.

He started when he realised her glass was empty. He lifted the bottle towards her in a silent question.

She hesitated and then held it out. 'Half a glass would be lovely.'

'I think you've done a great job with Robbie and Chase, Quinn. They're great kids. You should be proud of yourself.'

'Thank you.'

When she smiled at him he had to fight the urge to reach across and place his lips on hers. He closed his eyes and hauled in a breath. Kissing her wouldn't help. He forced his eyes open again. 'Do you ever regret the path you chose?'

'No, I don't. And I'm sure that's made things easier.' She turned to him more fully on the blanket. 'Remember how I said love makes everything easier?'

He nodded.

'Well, that goes for all love, not just romantic love. I love the boys with everything I have. They make it all worthwhile.'

Had she had to sacrifice all her dreams, though? 'What were you going to study at university?'

'Science. I was a major science geek.'

He recalled the science texts in her car. 'Is that why you chose to work in a science department at the university?'

'You bet. It meant I got to live vicariously through the research going on there. It was fun.'

His heart ached at the fierceness of her smile.

'But enough about me.' She dusted off her hands. 'I have a couple of questions of my own.'

He swallowed and shrugged. 'Ask away. After everything you've just shared, the least I can do is answer a couple of questions.'

She laughed and it flowed through him like some kind of energy drink. 'Careful, you might regret that impulse.'

What was it about her that could lift his spirits so instantly and comprehensively? 'Do your worst,' he dared on a laugh.

Slowly she sobered. She leaned in towards him. 'Aidan, why are you standing for office if you don't want to be a politician?'

CHAPTER SIX

AIDAN STARED AT Quinn and reminded himself to keep breathing.

How did she know?

His heart thumped. Perspiration prickled his scalp. He forced himself to sit up straighter and to lean away from her and the temptation of warm lips…of warm woman. 'Of course I want to be a politician.'

The sparkle in her eyes faded. 'Uh-huh.' She set her half glass of wine to one side and started to rise. 'It's been a lovely day, but a long one.'

She was going to leave? But she hadn't finished her wine! He didn't want the day to end, but he had no intention of talking about this.

'I hadn't thought it through properly, but of course you'd be worried I'd take such a story to the papers.'

'I think no such thing!'

Her face was a study in scepticism. 'Goodnight, Aidan, sleep tight.'

He scowled. He'd given her and her children a lovely day. Why did she have to push this?

Oh, so this day was more for their benefit than yours, was it?

He scowled harder, but Quinn didn't see. She was halfway back to her van by now.

And he didn't want her to go.

'When my brother died...'

She didn't turn, but she stopped. She didn't come back. She waited. He swallowed and tried to match his voice to the quiet of the night. 'I already told you that Danny's death devastated my parents.' A beat passed. 'Everything changed!'

She came back and sat on the blanket. She didn't pick up her wine glass. She didn't touch him. She didn't say a word.

He wanted her to say something—needed her to—because a lump had lodged in his throat and he couldn't push past it.

'What about you, Aidan? You must've been devastated too. You obviously loved your brother.'

The warm cadence of her voice helped him to relax, eased his throat muscles. 'I...' He ignored his wine to seize a bottle of water. He knocked back a generous swig. 'You have to understand that Danny was full of life, full of fun. If you were feeling low you could rely on Danny to cheer you up. You always found yourself laughing around him. He was the life of the party without being a party animal.' He capped the water bottle. 'When he died it felt like the light had gone out of the world.'

He hadn't said that out loud before. It wasn't something designed to cheer his mother or father, or anyone else for that matter. Quinn shuffled closer until their arms and shoulders touched. She took his hand. Strangely, her warmth did give him a measure of comfort.

'I always wanted a brother or sister. I can't imagine what it would be like to lose one I loved.'

Lost? They hadn't lost him. He'd been taken from them. Stolen. But it occurred to him then that he had memories Quinn would never have. Memories he could hold tight for the rest of his life. Something inside him shifted and changed focus by several degrees. He wanted to put his arm around her and hug her. He'd lost a brother, but he'd never been alone the way she had been.

'I was at a loss how to console my parents. Daniel wouldn't have been.'

She pulled herself up to her full sitting height. He'd slumped so the top of her shoulder almost came to the top of his. Although he should be focusing on other things, he couldn't help but enjoy the warm slide of her against him.

'Aidan Fairhall, you can't know that! You cannot possibly know how much Danny would've been affected if circumstances had been reversed. He might've gone completely to pieces.'

He shook his head. Danny would've known exactly how to comfort their parents. Besides, although none of them had said it out loud, they all knew his parents wouldn't have needed as much consoling if his and Danny's positions had been reversed.

That fact could still make him flinch.

Quinn's hold on his hand hauled him back. 'What does Danny's death have to do with you giving up a career you love and becoming a politician?'

He'd been foolish to think this woman had been fully preoccupied with her cross-country move and her two energetic sons. She'd picked up on a lot. Probably too much. 'Danny was always going to be the politician.' He moistened his lips. 'As you probably realise, Fairhalls always stand for office.'

'Your father, his father and his father before

him, yes, but nobody could've foreseen what happened to Danny.'

He met her gaze. The light of the fire glimmered in her eyes. 'The only thing that brought my parents a moment of respite and consolation was my promise to stand for office in Danny's place.'

Her lips parted. Her eyes and their sympathy burned through him. 'Oh, Aidan,' she whispered. 'Would it have been such a bad thing if it skipped a generation?'

He set his jaw. 'It might not be my first career choice, and I realise I'm probably going to make a dreadful politician, but—'

'No you won't! You'll be very good at it.'

He closed his eyes.

'But it'll be such a tough job if your heart isn't in it.'

He opened his eyes again. 'So I'm left with a choice that's really no choice at all. Either quit politics and break my parents' hearts all over again or reconcile myself to a job I have no real passion for.'

She swore. It was low and soft, but he caught it all the same and it made him swing towards her, his eyebrows lifting.

'Sorry,' she murmured. 'I just realised I'd made things ten times worse when I suggested you drag your mother into the office to help out with your campaign.'

That had sealed the deal. Not that there'd been much hope of pulling back now anyway. None of that was Quinn's fault.

'I think you're making a big mistake, Aidan.'

He shrugged. When a person got right down to it, what did his happiness count in the greater scheme of things? Besides, he wouldn't be miserable. He just wouldn't be following the path he'd choose for himself. It was no biggie.

His shoulders slumped.

'It wouldn't all go to hell in a hand basket if you were to retire from the campaign,' she argued, squeezing his hand. 'There are people who could step into your shoes, like your second in command.'

He appreciated her efforts, but she didn't understand how fragile his parents were.

'And you're not being fair to Daniel.'

Every muscle he possessed stiffened. He swung to her, a snarl rising up inside him. 'Not fair to Daniel? When I'm keeping his memory alive?'

She stared at him with wide eyes. She dropped his hand and it left him feeling strangely adrift. 'We keep our loved one's memory alive by remembering them and talking about them. Not by making a mockery of what they held dear.'

He bared his teeth. 'A mockery?'

'Well, what would you call it?' Her eyes flashed. 'He loved politics, yes? While you...you're just going to grit your teeth and force yourself to go through the motions. How do you think he'd feel about that, huh?'

Bile rose up through him.

'On a personal level, if he was any kind of brother at all, I bet he'd tell you to do whatever made you happy. On a professional level he would kick your butt for using the job he loved to make yourself and two other people feel marginally better.'

His jaw dropped. His stomach churned.

'Because he'd know politics is more important than that. Or, at least, that it should be. And he'd also know that you stepping into his shoes wouldn't bring him back.'

His head rocked back. Wind roared in his ears. His every last defence had been ripped away in one scalding wrench. He struggled to his feet, but he didn't know what to do once he'd reached them.

Flee?

Stand and fight?

Won't bring him back.

What he wanted to do was punch something and then hide in the dark and bawl his goddamn eyes out!

He backed up to lean against a nearby boulder outside the circle of light cast by the dying embers of the fire. Bracing his hands against his knees, he tried to pull air into lungs that didn't want to work.

He didn't hear her move, but suddenly she was there, insinuating herself between his legs, her arms going about his shoulders.

He couldn't help it. His arms went about her and he pulled her against him tight, his face buried in her shoulder.

Won't bring him back. But he wanted Danny back. He wanted it with his every aching atom, with every single, secret part of himself.

'You don't know what it's like, Quinn.' His voice came out raw and ragged. 'The pain...it tears at you from the inside out and you make deals with a God you don't believe in any more just to make it stop for five minutes. You'll do anything to try and get it to stop, to ease it a little bit, but...' Nothing worked. Not for long.

'I know, baby,' she crooned, cradling his head against her as she would if he were Chase or Robbie.

Won't bring him back.

He started to shake. A great hulking sob tore at his throat. Claws, cruel and vicious, raked at the parts of him he'd tried to protect, savage jaws closing about tender flesh as teeth, keen and sadistic, bit at him. A black pit opened up. A great scream roared in his ears. And all he could do was groan in grief and denial as night enclosed him, inside and out.

He didn't think he would ever be able to find his way out of it—out of the darkness—but faintly, ever so faintly, he heard Quinn's voice and he tried to focus on it, tried to move towards it. And eventually the shaking eased and the pain moved back a fraction and he could breathe again.

Slowly, the warmth of Quinn, the comfort of holding someone close, of having them hold him close, seeped through, pushing the darkness back further and further.

Finally he lifted his head. He wiped his eyes

and said the rudest word he knew. Quinn didn't flinch. Beyond her, in the sky, he could see a thousand stars.

He swore again. 'I just bawled like a great big baby, didn't I?'

'Oh, for heaven's sake.' She moved to sit beside him. He missed her warmth but he realised then that he'd been the first to let go. 'You're not going to come over all macho and tell me real men don't cry, are you?'

He blinked.

'For heaven's sake, how outdated are you? That is one message I won't be passing onto Chase and Robbie. You're human, right? Men feel just as deeply about things as women. Or are you going to tell me all men are shallow brutes?'

Nope. They weren't. Well, not most of them anyway, though he had serious doubts about Phillip.

'Bottling up grief like that makes everything bad. It doesn't let us keep hold of the stuff that's good.'

'What's good to be had from crying like that?' he muttered.

Even in the dark he could tell she'd fixed him

with a 'look'. He found himself having to fight a smile.

She jumped up, refilled their glasses and handed him one. 'You told me Danny was full of life, the life of the party and all that. Give me a specific example.'

He blinked. He opened his mouth and closed it again. He took a sip of wine and found it soothed his throat. A sigh sneaked out of him. One example of Danny's fun-ness, huh?

The first memory hit him. Then a second. And then they flooded him, one after the other. Nights at the local with their mates. Fishing trips. Surfing. Lots of laughing. Fights that had ended in laughter too. Barbecues. Late night talks sitting over a nice bottle of single malt.

He glanced at Quinn. She smiled and he found he could smile back without any effort at all. He knew then that he didn't have to relay a single one of those memories—she knew. How? He thought about all she'd been through and promptly stopped wondering.

'You must be tired.'

Her words were a caress in the night. 'You'd think so.' She'd barely touched her wine. He suspected she wasn't used to drinking. 'But I'm not.'

He felt oddly invigorated. Besides, it couldn't be much more than nine-thirty. 'Danny and I used to have these late night talks. We'd discuss how we were going to save the world—him the politician and me the human rights lawyer.'

The human rights lawyer.

'Sounds nice.'

His chest clenched. So did his hand. 'You're right, you know? He wouldn't want me living his dream.' Danny had possessed a heart as big as the Great Australian Bight. 'He'd have wanted me to follow my own dreams.' Danny had always cheered him from the sidelines.

'I wish I'd known him. He sounds like a great guy.'

It was the perfect thing to say. They stared at the stars for a while. 'My parents won't see it that way, though.'

'No.'

It was half-question, half-statement.

She leant against him, shoulder to shoulder. 'Are you going to try?'

'I think I have to.' But how? His mother's pale, haggard face and haunted eyes rose in his mind. Who did he most owe his allegiance to—his parents or Danny?

'You owe it to yourself,' Quinn said quietly, and he realised he'd spoken his thought out loud.

He didn't trust that, though. Following his dream, doing what he wanted seemed wrong and selfish in the circumstances. Yet it was the path Danny would have urged him to take.

'I take it your mother has been depressed, lethargic, hard to rouse?'

He nodded, his heart heavy again. Helping out on his campaign had certainly roused her, though.

'Have you ever considered the idea that behaving badly might rouse her more effectively than toeing the line?'

His glass halted halfway to his mouth. He slanted her a sidelong look. 'What are you talking about?'

She lifted one shoulder. 'If your mother thought that in your grief you were going off the rails…'

'It'd only add to her worries.' Surely?

'Or it might give her something different to worry about—something she could actually act on and make a difference to.'

She couldn't do anything about Danny's death,

she couldn't bring him back, but she could certainly pull Aidan back into line.

'There's a thread of deviousness in you, isn't there?'

'I know.'

She puffed out her chest and it made him laugh. 'What did you have in mind?'

'Well, I was thinking that maybe when you reach Adelaide, rather than catch the first available flight back to Sydney, what if you were seen out on the town, gambling and drinking? I'm not saying to actually do those things, but if it appeared as if you were...'

Quinn watched the implication of her idea ripple behind the smooth dark amber of Aidan's eyes.

'She'd be livid.'

'Livid could be good,' she offered. 'It's better than apathy.'

'If I could somehow help her remember the good stuff too...'

He turned to her and his face was so vulnerable in the starlight she wanted to hug him. He was such a good man. 'She won't forget her grief, Aidan. Just like you won't forget yours.' They'd carry it always and there'd still be bad days. She hoped he knew that. 'But hopefully she'll learn to live with it.'

'You helped me get rid of something dark and heavy inside me, Quinn, that I didn't even realise I was carrying around.'

'You'd been pushing your grief back to focus on your parents' needs instead.' No wonder he'd been ready to explode. Who'd been looking after his needs?

'And you think if I force my mother to focus on me instead of her grief, that it might help her?'

'I don't know. I don't know your mother, but I thought it might be worth a try. What do you think?'

He stared at the fire. 'I think it might be worth a try too.' He cocked an eyebrow at her. 'Going off the rails, huh?'

He grinned. It made her heart chug. She set down her glass. The wine was obviously going to her head.

'You left out one important element in your little "going off the rails" scenario, Quinn.'

'What's that?'

'An inappropriate woman draped on my arm.'

His grin deepened and she knew she was in

trouble. She did what she could to swallow back a knot of excitement. 'Do you really think that's necessary?'

'Absolutely! Drinking, gambling and carousing with wild women won't do my campaign any good.'

She stared at him.

'What?' he eventually said.

'You seem to think your mother will only be worried about your campaign and the damage you might do to it.'

He glanced away.

Didn't he think his mother would be worried about him on a personal level? She understood that some people found it hard to separate the personal and professional, but what did a job matter when it came to a loved one's mental and emotional health and their—?

She broke off, remembering the world he came from—a world where duty and position and prominence were more important than loving your family.

'If I'm going to do this, Quinn, I mean to do it big.'

So he couldn't turn back? She understood that—way down deep inside her in a place she didn't want to look at too closely. He wanted to give his mother an almighty jolt *and* he wanted to sabotage his campaign at the same time. Two birds. One stone. She felt suddenly uneasy, though she couldn't explain why.

'Will you help me?'

'You want me to be that wild woman on your arm?'

'Yes.'

She wasn't opposed to helping him. She and the boys had plenty of time to dilly-dally. 'Tell me what it would entail.'

He drummed his fingers against his thigh. 'It'd mean spending a couple of nights carousing on the town. So...three nights all up in Adelaide.'

'Okay.' That was manageable. 'What about the boys? I don't want them in the papers.' She and Aidan wouldn't make front-page headlines, but they'd make the social pages.

'We can shield them. And we can do fun stuff with them through the day too,' he added, unprompted. It turned her heart to jelly. 'There's a zoo. And I bet they'd love the Adelaide Gaol Museum, not to mention the Haigh's Chocolate visitor centre. And there's this fabulous aquatic centre with slides and caves and all sorts of things.'

He cared about making her boys happy. She knew then that she wouldn't be able to refuse him.

Not that you ever intended to.

'We'll stay somewhere upmarket that has a babysitting service.' He straightened and pinned her with his gaze. 'And I'll be covering all the expenses in Adelaide. That's non-negotiable.'

She rolled her eyes. 'I'm not exactly penniless, you know? I have enough to cover it.'

'You might not be penniless, but you're understandably careful with your money. Besides, given the choice, you wouldn't stay in an upmarket motel. Also, you're doing this as a favour to me so I'm paying.'

She planted her hands on her hips. 'On one condition.'

'Shoot.'

'That you don't pay for my car rental.' He'd paid for all of their fuel so far and she'd figured that was a good enough deal.

He'd started to turn away but he swung back. 'How'd you know I was going to do that?'

'Oh, Aidan Fairhall, you are as see-through as glass.'

He thrust his jaw out. 'I am not!'

She just laughed.

His jaw lowered. 'All right then, *you* might see through me but most people don't.'

She'd give him that. Most people, she suspected, only saw what they wanted where Aidan was concerned.

'Okay,' he grumbled. 'You have yourself a deal.'

He held out his hand. She placed hers in it and they shook on it. He didn't release her. 'Thank you, Quinn. I can't begin to tell you how much I appreciate it.'

She opened her mouth to tell him to try, but realised that might be construed as flirting. Her reckless self lifted its head and stretched. She cleared her throat. 'You're welcome.'

One side of his mouth hooked up in a slow, slightly wicked smile. He still held her hand. 'I'm looking forward to hitting the town with you.'

She should pull her hand free. 'Why?'

He tugged her a little closer and her reckless side shimmied. 'Do you dance?'

Her breath caught in her chest, making her heart thud. 'Like you wouldn't believe.'

'I'm better,' he promised.

'We'll see about that.'

'What's your favourite cocktail?'

'A Margarita. Yours?'

'A whiskey sour.'

His thumb caressed the soft skin at her wrist. 'Can you play blackjack?'

'With the best of them.' The nearest she'd come to gambling was the odd flutter on the Melbourne Cup. 'Although I prefer roulette.'

'I'm going to take you out dancing and gambling and drinking.'

'And I'm going to hang off your arm and gaze up at you adoringly. And I'm going to laugh and tease you and be every kind of a temptress I can think of.' His mother would have a fit.

'And I'm going to kiss you.'

And then his mouth came down on hers in the dark of the night, hot and demanding, and it stole her breath. His kiss wasn't polite or quiet. It was dark and thrilling and she threw all sense of caution to the wind, winding her arms about his neck and kissing him back.

He pulled her in closer, trapping her between lean, powerful thighs, and deepened the kiss. She didn't resist. His hands curved about her hips and explored them completely, boldly and oh-so-impolitely. She moved against him restlessly as the thrill became a dark throb in her blood. Thrusting her hands into his hair, she held him still to thoroughly explore a mouth that set her on fire, inciting him to further bold explorations of her body with hands that seemed to know exactly what she craved.

Aidan's kiss made her feel impulsive and young.

It made her feel beautiful.

It made her feel like a woman.

She wanted him, fiercely and deeply, as if his lovemaking would be an antidote to some secret hidden pain she carried inside her.

She broke off to gulp air into starved lungs. His lips found her throat—no butterfly whispers here, just hot, wet grazes and suckles that built the inferno growing inside her. His hands were beneath her dress. They were beneath her panties, cupping her bare buttocks, kneading and pleasing and building that inferno. Her hands went to the waistband of his shorts—

Wait.

No, no, she didn't want to wait. She wanted to lose herself in sheer sensation. She wanted to forget her troubles and soar away in mindless and delirious pleasure. Oh, please let her…

Ask the question.

She froze. Aidan's clever, heat-inducing, plea-sure-seeking fingers started to move and she knew that in a moment she would be lost. To-tally and completely.

With a groan of pure frustration, she slapped her hands over the top of his, the fabric of her dress between them.

He stared up at her. 'Oh, God, Quinn. Please don't pull back now.'

'I have to ask a question.'

'Ask away.' His breathing was as ragged and uneven as hers.

'Not of you, of me.'

She pulled his hands out from beneath her dress. She stumbled back over to the blanket and lowered herself to it, drawing up her knees and wrapping her arms around them. Aidan didn't move. She could still taste him on her tongue. She needed a drink of water, but she didn't want to wash the taste of him away.

'What's the question, Quinn?'

The question scared the beejeebies out of her. 'Would I be prepared to fall pregnant to you?'

Although the fire was now completely out, she saw the way he rocked back at her words. She didn't blame him.

'You see, twice now I've fallen pregnant without meaning to. When precautions had been
taken. So I've had to make this my default position.' It played havoc with her sex life.

Her non-existent sex life.

He came to sit on the blanket too. But not too
close. 'Wow.'

'You should ask it of yourself too—would you
be prepared to make love with me if it would re-
sult in me getting pregnant?'

She couldn't read his eyes. She suddenly
laughed. 'Boy, wouldn't that throw a spanner in
your campaign?'

He didn't laugh.

'But I don't think we want to scare your mother
that much.'

'Quinn...'

When he didn't go on she pulled in a breath.
'I like babies and I like you, Aidan, but I'm not
prepared to get pregnant to you.' She would never
again give a man the chance to accuse her of ruining his life.

He moved in closer. 'We wouldn't have to...
you know. We could improvise, set boundaries
and rules.'

She edged back. 'No, we couldn't. That kind of

passion—' she gestured over towards the boulder '—is dangerous. Boundaries get crossed and rules get broken. And in the heat of the moment neither one of us would care.'

And she'd woken up before to the cold, hard light of day.

'Maybe I'd risk it if I'd been on the Pill for three months and had a diaphragm and spermicide cream with me and you used a condom, but...'

'I don't even have a condom!' He sat back with a curse. She didn't blame him.

'Aidan, if you want me to play the role of wild woman in Adelaide then you have to promise me that won't happen again.'

Even in the darkness she could see the way his eyes narrowed. 'Why not?'

She could almost see his mind ticking over—there were condoms and diaphragms and spermicide creams and any number of things available in the city.

'Because we're from different worlds, that's why not. We—us—are not going to happen. It can't go anywhere.'

'What the hell are you talking about?'

'You're all corporate meetings and flash hotel suites. I'm P & C committees and bedtime stories.'

'Lawyers and politicians have kids.'

'Not with me, they don't.' Not when they worked eighty-hour weeks. 'What would your parents say?'

That shut him up. She twisted her hands together. 'I mean after Adelaide we won't even see each other again.'

'So we're not even friends?'

Friends? She swallowed. 'We're just ships in the night.'

'Without the benefits,' he bit out and she had to close her eyes and give her reckless self a stern talking to.

'Adelaide,' she croaked. 'Are we on the same page?'

He didn't say anything for a long moment. Finally he nodded. 'Publicly affectionate but hands off in private.'

A quick kiss dropped to the lips or pressed to the cheek was very different to—

Don't think about it!

'I'm glad that's settled.' But she had to force the words out from between gritted teeth.

CHAPTER SEVEN

TWO DAYS LATER, Quinn stretched out on the five-star comfort of a queen bed and let out a low satisfied groan. She, the boys and Aidan had spent the majority of the day at the aquatic park. The boys had had a blast on the water slides. So had Aidan.

And so had she, though she didn't doubt for a single moment that she deserved a mid-afternoon rest. Somehow she'd managed to keep her hands to herself and her mind mostly on the boys rather than with fantasies filled with Aidan, which was no small feat considering he'd been parading around in his board shorts for most of the day.

Robbie abandoned his Gameboy to climb up onto the bed beside her. The door to the boys' adjoining twin room stood wide open. Rather than watch television in their own room, however, they'd chosen to settle in her room to play their Gameboys.

'It's been the funnest day,' he said, nestling in beside her.

'It has, hasn't it?'

'Is there a water park in Pokolbin?'

She shook her head and watched carefully to see if his face fell. It did a bit.

Chase climbed up onto the bed too. 'I love holidays! What are we going to do tomorrow?'

She opened her free arm so he could snuggle in against her too. 'Well, now, if you two let me have a sleep-in, maybe we could see our way to visiting the zoo.'

Both boys started to bounce.

A knock sounded on the door. Before she could move, a voice on the other side called out, 'It's Aidan.'

'Come on in,' she called back. Reclining on her bed probably wasn't the best place to receive visitors—especially one as alluring as Aidan—but she did have the safeguard of two young boys tucked in at her sides and they'd banish anything loaded from the situation.

When he saw them, Aidan's grin hooked up one side of his mouth. 'That rest you said you were going to take...' He glanced at the bouncing, wide-awake boys. 'It looks...uh...successful.'

She forced her eyes wide. 'Oh, yes.'

They both laughed.

Chase launched himself off the bed and across to Aidan. 'Mum said we might go to the zoo to-morrow.'

Aidan lounged in the doorway, all hot, relaxed male, and it made her stomach tighten and her breath shorten.

'But only if we let her have a sleep-in first.' Robbie joined them in the doorway.

'That sounds like a fair exchange.' Aidan glanced at her and she suddenly realised she was alone, adrift on this enormous bed. He sucked his bottom lip into his mouth and his eyes darkened.

She hitched herself up higher against the head-board and made sure her dress covered her legs to below her knees. She avoided direct eye con-tact, but couldn't stop herself from looking in his direction. He bent down to whisper something to the boys. They glanced at her with barely con-tained excitement and raced off to their room.

And then Quinn found herself alone in all of this five-star luxury with Aidan, and she couldn't move a muscle. It took all of her strength to wres-tle the fantasies rising through her to the ground.

'I hope you're not going to be upset by what I've just organised.'

She had to get off this bed!

She swung her legs over the side, forced steel to watery knees and moved across the room to one of a pair of tub chairs. She motioned for Aidan to take the other but he remained lounging in the doorway and she suddenly realised he didn't trust himself to come any further into the room.

Heat scorched her cheeks. A whimper rose inside her. She cleared her throat. 'What have you organised?'

'An afternoon of pampering for you while I take the boys to the movies.'

'Oh! Oh, that sounds divine, but...'

'Please don't refuse. You put everyone else's needs before your own and...' He folded his arms. 'I wanted to thank you. I really appreciate what you're doing for me.'

'You've repaid me tenfold by helping me give the boys a holiday they'll never forget.'

'I'm enjoying it as much as they are.'

So was she.

'So...?'

There was something in his eyes, something hopeful and happy that she didn't want to wound.

Pampering? She smoothed her dress down over her knees and lifted one shoulder, glancing at him sideways over it. 'What exactly have you organised?' What kind of *pampering* were they talking about here?

'A massage, a facial, a manicure, a pedicure and a stylist for your hair and make-up.'

Her eyes widened. She did her best not to drool.

'And someone from the hotel boutique will be up with a variety of outfits for you to choose from for tonight.'

'Oh, that's too much!'

'It's not half of what you deserve.'

'But...'

'Look, Quinn, I suspect you'd rather just stay in and watch a DVD with the boys than hit the town tonight.'

Then he thought wrong.

'So I'm trying to make this as pleasant for you as possible.'

She really should say no.

'I suspect you don't have anything appropriate in your suitcase to wear for this evening— it wasn't the kind of trip you had planned—and I don't want to put you to unnecessary expense and the bother of having to go out at short notice to buy something.'

It was true. She didn't have a single thing in her suitcase that would do. She'd been hoping to dash out to buy something. And there was still time, but...

She should've known he'd have taken all of this into account. The allure of a few hours all to herself circled around her, warm with promise. She hadn't had the kind of pampering Aidan was proposing since the afternoon of her eighteenth birthday party. 'I should refuse.'

'There are no strings.'

She smiled. She already knew that. 'I really should refuse, but I'm afraid your offer is far too tempting. It sounds heavenly, Aidan. Thank you for thinking of it.'

He grinned at her. Her heart started to thump. She moistened her lips. 'I'll just make sure the boys are ready to go to the movies.'

She started to rise, but a hand on her shoulder kept her in her seat. 'Leave the boys to me. I'll collect you for dinner at seven-thirty.'

And then he was through the adjoining door into the boys' room with the door between them firmly closed, as if he'd been afraid to linger.

She hugged herself. He was taking her hands-off policy seriously and it touched her, made her feel safe. Even as it left her body clamouring with frustration.

Quinn swung from surveying herself in the full-length mirror to answer the knock from the adjoining door. The boys' babysitter stood on the other side—a fresh-faced eighteen-year-old with a wide smile and a winning manner.

'Robbie and Chase want to say goodnight.'

'I'll come through.' She went to step into the room but Holly didn't move. She just stared at Quinn. Quinn swallowed and ran a hand across the electric-blue knit of her dress. 'What do you think?'

'I think you look hot!' Holly straightened. 'Oh, I mean—'

'No, no.' Quinn laughed. 'That was perfect.'

Both boys' eyes widened when she walked into their room. 'You look beautiful,' Robbie breathed.

'Beautifuller than beautiful,' Chase whispered.

She kissed them both, told them to be good for Holly, double-checked that the sitter had her mobile number, and then moved back into her own room to pace. That was three votes in the pro camp so far, but Aidan's was the vote that counted.

Would he think she looked 'hot' and 'beautiful'?

She sank down to the bed and lifted a leg out to admire her strappy black sandals. A bow studded with diamantés sat high at each ankle. These were definitely wild woman shoes.

A glance at the clock told her she still had five minutes before Aidan would arrive. She checked her hair in the mirror. It had been swept up into a loose French roll. A couple of tendrils curled by her ears to brush her shoulders and neck. It was an elegant style to counter the sexiness of her dress and shoes and the glitter of dangling diamantés in her ears. She hoped Aidan would approve.

She stepped back to survey her overall image again. Oh, Lord! What if she'd gone too far and—?

A knock sounded.

She swung to stare at the closed door. Her fingers curved around her stomach to try and counter its crazy churning. She suddenly wished herself next door with the boys, watching whatever movie it was that they'd chosen.

There was another knock.

Oh, get over yourself!

She kicked herself forward and opened the door. Aidan stood there in black trousers and a white shirt with a black jacket casually tossed over one shoulder. Her mouth dried. He looked...

Divine. Scrumptious. Sexy.

And like a stranger.

She held her breath and waited for him to smile.

His gaze swept her from the top of her French roll to the tips of her ruby-coloured toenails, and back again. Her blood thundered in her ears.

His eyes flashed and his lips pressed into a thin, hard line. Her heart slithered to her knees. She wanted to close the door and hide behind it, but she forced her chin skyward.

'We'd best go if we don't want to be late.' Clipped and short, the words shot out of him like arrows, barbed and flinty.

'I'll just get my purse.'

She turned, blinking hard against the stinging in her eyes.

Aidan punched the elevator button and kept his eyes firmly fixed straight ahead.

Damn it! He should've arranged to meet Quinn

in the foyer. It would've been a heck of a lot safer. What had he been thinking? He tried to slow the tempo of the blood in his veins. He tried to remember to keep breathing. In out. In out. He gritted his teeth. It wasn't hard.

The elevator doors slid open on a silent whoosh. He motioned Quinn ahead of him, careful not to touch her. He caught a glimpse of long tanned thigh and swallowed a groan.

Pull yourself together. He'd seen more of her body at the aquatic centre earlier in the day. He slammed a finger to the button for the ground floor. *Hurry up*! He didn't need a confined space at this point in time. He'd made her a promise—a promise he wouldn't break. His hands clenched. But all he could see from the corner of his eyes was a vibrant tempting blue.

Her swimsuit had been a simple one-piece designed for modesty. The dress she wore now was anything but. It was flamboyant and provocative. And those heels! She was wearing take-me-to-bed shoes. What he wouldn't give to do exactly that and—

Nostrils flaring, he forced his gaze straight ahead to the polished metal of the elevator doors. He stared at them, willed them to open onto the ground floor asap and deposit them into a crowd and safety.

'I'm sorry, Aidan.' Quinn pushed the button to halt the elevator's progress. 'But I can't do this. I can't go out if what I'm wearing is inappropriate.'

He turned. She'd caught her bottom lip between her teeth, but not before he'd seen its betraying wobble. He closed his eyes and tried to collect himself, resisting the urge to run a finger around his collar. 'Quinn, what you're wearing is perfect for this evening and—'

'You hate it.'

He'd hurt her feelings? *Careless brute!* 'I love it!'

'No, you—'

'But I'm in danger of forgetting my promise to you so I'm trying to get us out of the danger zone as quickly as I can.'

She blinked. Not an ounce of comprehension dawned in her eyes. He leaned in closer. 'At the moment all I want to do is haul you back to your room, toss you onto your bed like some darn caveman and to slowly and very thoroughly explore every—'

Her hand clapped over his mouth. 'I get the picture.' Her voice came out hoarse and she pressed the button to set the elevator in motion again. 'Sorry, I thought…'

She brought her hand back. 'I've never worn anything this risqué before and I thought maybe I'd taken the whole wild woman thing too far. I mean, look how short this hem is! Not to mention that this material hugs every curve, leaving next to nothing to the imagination.'

He closed his eyes again.

'And now I'm rambling. Sorry. Nerves. I have to try to get your suggestion out of my head or…'

He bit back a groan.

'Not that what you suggested would work in practice.'

He opened his eyes and raised an eyebrow.

'I mean, the minute the boys heard we were back they'd be straight into my room and I expect that would be something of a mood killer.'

He laughed then. He couldn't help it. The door whooshed open and he took her hand to stride out into the foyer. He said now what he should've said at her door. 'Sweetheart, you look absolutely ravishing. I am going to be the envy of every man that claps eyes on you tonight.'

She beamed back at him. 'We're going to have so much fun this evening.'

They would. Just as long as he remembered the promise he'd made. And kept reminding himself that he was a man of his word.

Quinn was right. Dinner was fun.

She recounted the pampering she'd received that afternoon, and her sheer enjoyment of it touched him. Life had been unkind to Quinn, but she didn't waste time feeling sorry for herself. She took full responsibility for her own happiness. Still, it felt good to have given her a treat.

'Have dessert,' he urged. 'I mean to.'

She shook her head. 'I couldn't possibly fit it in. But I'd love a coffee.'

That made him grin. 'Not used to late nights, Ms Laverty?'

Her eyes danced. 'Not ones that don't involve earaches or tummy upsets.' She glanced around. 'I have to say, Aidan, this is a really lovely restaurant.'

They sat at a window table that overlooked Adelaide's streetscape. The lights of the city twinkled beneath them with an effervescence he found infectious.

He ordered coffee for Quinn and chocolate mousse cake for himself. When the waiter had gone, Quinn turned from the view to survey him. 'So...how will the press know that you're out on the town tonight?'

'They've been tipped off.'

'Right.'

'When we leave here there'll be a photographer somewhere. He could be hidden or he could be brash and in our faces.'

'If it's the latter, how should I act? Natural or furtive?'

He considered that. 'It won't matter.' Either would garner his mother's full attention. 'And there'll be more of the same at the nightclub we're going to.' He'd arranged for a photographer to get in and take photos of him and Quinn dancing. He didn't tell her that, though. He didn't want her feeling self-conscious the entire evening.

She stared out of the window with pursed lips and he frowned. 'What's the matter?'

'I'm feeling a little uneasy...'

'You don't need to. I promise to look after you and—'

'About doing all this to sabotage your campaign.'

He was prevented from answering when the waiter arrived with dessert and coffee.

'But that's the whole point of the exercise,' he said when the waiter was gone.

'The point is to rouse your mother from her depression and make her look beyond her grief.' She reached out and touched his hand. 'Why can't you just tell your parents the truth—that you don't want to be a politician?'

How could he tell Quinn that her plan was a losing game? His parents loved him, sure, but it had never been on the same scale as they'd loved Danny. Besides, he didn't want to have that particular conversation with his mother. It wouldn't be a conversation but an argument. It would end in her tears and his guilt. Lose-lose. This way...

'Aidan?'

The lights of the city were reflected in her eyes and it made something inside him start to pound. He swallowed and tried to ignore it. 'If I tell my parents I don't want to embark on a political career they'll be mortally offended.'

She frowned.

'What they'd hear is not that I love my job as a human rights lawyer, but me criticizing their entire way of life and value system. What they'd hear is me *spurning* their way of life and all they hold dear. And most of all, Quinn, what they'd see is me refusing to bring Danny's dream to fruition.' He stared down at the chocolate cake, his appetite all used up. 'They'd see it as a betrayal.'

Her lips parted a fraction and her eyes almost seemed to throb. 'Oh, Aidan,' she whispered.

He ached to reach out and touch her.

'So instead you're going to let them devalue all you hold dear, to belittle the life you want to lead?'

'I can live with that. My losing the campaign will be a blow to them, a major disappointment, but it's always been on the cards. That's the nature of politics. But me walking away from it all, they would find that unforgivable.'

'What if you're wrong?'

A weight settled on his shoulders. What if they didn't forgive him for 'going off the rails' and *inadvertently* sabotaging his political career?

'What if you're short-changing them? It's possible that they'd understand your position, you know. They don't sound like ogres. You're not narrow-minded. Danny doesn't sound as if he was narrow-minded, which makes me think they're not either. You're not giving them a chance to support you.'

'Danny has only been gone for eight months.

I might not be prepared to sacrifice myself to a career in politics, but I'm not prepared to cause them any more pain than necessary. Not at this point in time.'

They stared at each other for several long moments and he clocked the exact instant she decided to leave it be. He should've been relieved, but he wasn't. Which didn't make any sense.

She reached across with her teaspoon and snared a spoonful of his cake. 'Oh, that is really good. I mean *seriously* good.' He went to push it towards her but she shook her head. 'The last thing you need is to be seen on the dance floor with a woman who has a distended stomach.'

Her wryness made him laugh. 'Quinn, when all of this is over, I'd like to keep seeing you.' Pokolbin was only two hours north of Sydney, maybe two and a half. It wasn't that far.

She snagged another spoonful of his cake and shook her head. 'Not going to happen.'

He forced himself to have a spoonful of cake too. Forced himself to hide how much her easy rejection cut at him. 'Why not?'

'Because I refuse to be a part of your strategy to ruin your political career. And we both know a woman like me—a single, unmarried mother

with a low-paying job and few qualifications—
is not the kind of woman to stand at an aspiring
politician's side.'

'That's not why I want to see you!'

'Maybe not.' She ate more cake and she looked
utterly in control but the spoon trembled in her
hand. 'But I remind you of Danny. I remind you
of better times and I wonder how much of the
real me you see.'

He flinched and abandoned all pretence of eating. 'You're just grasping after any excuse. You
want to deny what's happening between us.'

She set her teaspoon to her saucer. 'There's an
element of truth in that.'

Her simple statement made his jaw drop.

'You're a nice man, Aidan. I like you a lot,
but...' She glanced up and met his gaze. 'Honesty is important to me.'

A chill slid beneath his ribs.

'Phillip lied to me about what he really wanted
because he thought that was the right thing to do.
The same way that you're lying to your parents.'

Her words couldn't hurt him. His heart had
numbed and frozen over. 'You're saying you don't
trust me.'

'Are you saying you'd never lie to me?'

Of course he wouldn't! He could say that till he was blue in the face, though. She'd never believe it. Phillip had done a right royal job on her.

'Your actions speak louder, I'm afraid.'

His parents and his relationship with her were two different issues!

'I'm not some child that needs protecting and I refuse to ever be treated like that again.'

He sat back. He scowled at his cake. Quinn drained her coffee. 'Stop being so glum,' she chided. 'We're supposed to be having fun, remember? You promised me dancing.'

Quinn was running scared. That was what all this was about. He scrubbed a hand down his face. He had the rest of tonight, all day tomorrow and tomorrow night to work on her.

If he dared.

Aidan woke to the piercing ringtone of his mobile phone. He fumbled for it. 'Hello?' he mumbled.

'Aidan Carter Fairhall, have you seen the papers today?'

His eyes sprang open. 'Mum!' He sat bolt upright in bed. He dragged in a breath. Right. 'Hold on.'

He padded to the door of his room and opened

it. As requested, copies of all the national news-
papers awaited him. He scooped them up and
moved back to the bed. 'I have them all here.
Which one in particular were you referring to?'

'All of them!'

He flicked through to the society pages and
then grinned. Perfect. 'Ah...' He hemmed and
hawed, injecting what he desperately hoped
were notes of equivocation and vagueness into
his voice.

'What on earth did you think you were doing?'

'I was just having a bit of...fun.'

'You're practically pawing that woman in public!'

'She's a very nice woman.'

His mother snorted.

'Look, what's the big deal? I went out. I had
fun.' The irritation that edged into his voice
wasn't feigned.

'The big deal is that photographs like this—
where you look drunk, not to mention *lewd*—
will do untold damage to your political image!
What on earth do you think you were doing?' she
repeated as if she couldn't believe his stupidity.

He scrubbed a hand across his chin.

'Aidan?'

'Do you know how far it is across the Nullarbor, Mum?' Silence greeted him. 'And it's all just endless sand and scrub for mile upon weary mile. It gives a man time to think.'

'What do you mean?'

The wobble in his mother's voice made his gut clench. He wished he could've spared her all the pain she'd suffered in the last eight months. 'Ever since Danny…' He couldn't finish that sentence. 'For the last eight months I've thrown myself into work to try and forget, but it doesn't work like that, does it? I need a holiday. I'm *taking* a holiday.'

'You don't have time for a holiday! You can have a holiday once you've been elected to office. You listen to me, Aidan. You are going to haul your backside out of whatever seedy hotel it's currently residing in, you will say goodbye to your slutty little friend, and you will get yourself to the airport. *Now!* We have work to do if we're to minimise the damage you've already done.'

Slutty?

'Do you hear me?'

He thrust out his jaw. 'No.'

An indrawn breath reached him down the end of the phone. 'I beg your pardon?'

That tone had made him quail as a kid. A part of him was glad to hear it now. He hadn't heard his mother this riled in a long time. But Quinn *slutty*? 'No can do, Mum. I'm not ready to come home. I'll call you in a couple of days to let you know my plans.' And he cut the line.

They spent the day at the zoo.

Aidan took every opportunity that presented itself to touch Quinn—a hand in the small of her back at the turnstile and again in the queue for the canteen, a brushing of fingers when he handed her a drink, the touch of arms and shoulders as they sat on a bench for a rest, a hand at her elbow when they ascended some steps. The startled glitter in her eyes and the flush that developed high on her cheekbones had him biting back a groan, along with the urge to rush her off somewhere private.

He wanted her mind filled with the sight, smell and feel of him. He wanted it to plague her with the same insistence it gnawed at him. He wanted the frustration of unassuaged hunger to batter down all her defences until not a single one was left.

He didn't know how far he and Quinn could

cultivate their relationship but, presented with the stark fact of parting company with her tomorrow, he knew he had to try something.

She's a single mother. Leave her alone. This is just lust. Scratch that itch elsewhere.

He thrust out his chin. It went deeper than mere chemistry and it deserved to be explored.

Aren't you hurting your mother enough?

A fist clenched in his chest. This had nothing to do with his mother!

What would Danny tell you to do?

Everything stilled. His mind went blank.

'Will we get to see them eat?' Robbie asked as they moved towards the big cat area.

It had just been dinner time at the seal and dolphin enclosures. The boys had been fascinated.

'Not today,' Quinn said, reading a nearby sign.

Robbie pouted. 'Why not?'

'Because lions and tigers don't get fed every day. The zoo tries to mimic how they'd feed in the wild. It keeps them healthy.'

Aidan nudged her arm. She started. He bit back a grin. 'How'd you know that?'

'You'll be sorry you asked,' she warned.

He folded his arms. 'Go on.'

She shrugged. 'I've been reading up on some

of the latest research into human health and nutrition.' He raised an eyebrow and she shrugged. 'It appears that just as it's healthier for wild animals to intermittently fast, the same might be true for humans.'

His mind flicked back to those textbooks in her car.

'There are links that suggest fasting can decrease both the incidence and growth of some cancers, reduce the risk of developing diabetes, and perhaps even Alzheimer's. It appears that fasting could promote cell renewal. I mean, the research is only in its infancy, but it is fascinating.'

He listened in astonishment and then awe as she rattled off facts and figures with an ease that spoke of close scholarship. She eventually petered off with a shrug and an abashed grin that speared into his heart. 'I told you you'd be sorry.'

'It's amazing and interesting,' he countered. He thought of the way she'd just spoken, of the fire in her voice, of those darn textbooks and the lecture she'd given him that first day about his probable cortisol levels. He pulled her to a halt. 'Quinn, why are you wasting all of this passion and talent? Why aren't you at university, conducting your own research?'

She stared at him for a moment and then pointed—to Robbie and Chase.

Ah.

In the next instant he rallied. 'But there's nothing to stop you from going to university now.'

She glanced pointedly to Robbie and Chase again and then raised an eyebrow.

'You could study part-time. You'd get government assistance while you were studying and—'

'You mean I'd end up with a big fat student debt.'

'And a bright and shiny qualification.'

'Look, Aidan, I made my decision nine years ago when I found out I was pregnant. I have to work full-time to make ends meet, that's non-negotiable, and I'm also a full-time mum. Studying even part-time would mean spreading myself too thin. Robbie and Chase deserve more than my part-time distracted attention. They deserve at least one fully involved parent.'

He opened his mouth, but she held up a hand. 'Maybe I'll rethink that when the boys are in high school and a bit more self-sufficient.'

By which time he didn't doubt she'd have come

up with a whole new set of excuses. Her shuttered expression, though, told him the subject was closed.

That evening they went to Adelaide's night races.

Quinn instantly fell in love with the pageantry, the colour and the sheer excitement.

'Which one do you fancy?' Aidan asked her as the horses paraded in front of them.

'Number four,' she said, selecting a giant chestnut. The jockey wore the exact same shade as Aidan's shirt.

'Come on.' He took her hand and led her to one of the betting windows and handed her an obscene amount of cash. 'Put it all on the nose.'

'All?' she breathed.

He just grinned and it made her heart hammer. Heaven's, how on earth was she going to adjust to reality again tomorrow? When Aidan would be gone. For good.

She pushed the thought away. Tonight was for fun. There'd be time enough to miss all of this, to miss him, tomorrow.

She watched the race with her heart in her mouth, gripping Aidan's arm. As the horses hit the home straight she started jumping up and down and shouting along with the rest of the crowd, cheering on her horse with all her might. When number four crossed the finish line a nose ahead of the rest of the field, she flung her arms around Aidan's neck. 'We won! We won!'

He swung her around before setting her back on her feet and grinning down at her. She eased away, the hard imprint of his body burnt on her brain. Did she really mean to let this man go? 'I'm having the best time,' she breathed.

You don't have any choice.

'Me too.'

Live for today. Tomorrow will take care of itself. It wasn't a view she tended to subscribe to, but she threw herself into it wholeheartedly now.

Despite the heat that flared between them and its insidious insistence that throbbed deep in her blood, Quinn found herself laughing when she and Aidan entered the foyer of their hotel later that evening. Even the knowledge lurking at the corners of her consciousness that their fun was at an end couldn't prevent her from holding tight to these last precious moments.

The foyer was empty except for the concierge and a receptionist, and an elegant woman sitting stiffly in one of the easy chairs. Aidan froze when he saw her. Quinn frowned up at him, completely attuned to his mood. 'What is it?'

The woman rose, her chin tilted at a haughty angle. 'Hello, Aidan.'

Aidan turned to Quinn, his smile stiff. 'Quinn, this is my mother, Vera Fairhall.'

CHAPTER EIGHT

A<small>IDAN'S</small> <small>MOTHER</small>!

Quinn's eyes widened and her jaw slackened. One glance at the other woman and she decided not to offer her hand. She swallowed and did her best to push her shoulders back. 'How do you do?' she said. She didn't say, 'pleased to meet you'. She doubted she'd be able to pull that lie off.

Mrs Fairhall didn't reply. Beneath her chilly gaze, Quinn's flirty red skirt seemed too short and her cream silk singlet top too skimpy. Which, of course, was true on both counts. She wore her strappy black sandals again, the ones with the bows, and the look they received basically said, 'woman of the night shoes'.

She choked back a giggle. Oh, Lord, they were in the middle of a farce!

'And who is this, Aidan?'

Tension vibrated through him and Quinn's desire to giggle promptly fled. His eyes flashed and his hands clenched. All of his easy politeness had disappeared, leaving a deep, burning anger she found hard to associate with him. She curled her hand around his arm and squeezed, tried to silently transmit that he not do or say anything he'd regret later.

Eight months might've passed but he and his mother were still both in deep mourning. People did and said things they didn't mean when operating under such stress. And Aidan mightn't be drunk, but they had been drinking.

He stared down at her for a moment and his face relaxed, and then a gleam she didn't trust lit his eyes. He slipped his arm about her waist and pulled her in close to his side. 'Mum, I'd like you to meet Quinn Laverty, the woman I mean to marry.'

The foyer spun. Quinn sagged against Aidan's side. She kept her eyes firmly fixed on the floor, knowing if she didn't they'd betray her. She closed them. What did he think he was doing? She should bring this lie to a close. It wouldn't do any of them any good, not in the long run.

'You expect me to congratulate you?'

He coiled up as if he were ready to spring. She leaned against him harder to keep him where he stood.

'Just once it'd be nice to hear you congratulate me on something that actually mattered to me.'

The words might've been drawled, but she sensed the very real pain beneath them. An innate loyalty for this man shot to the fore. 'Aidan,' she chided. 'We weren't going to tell anybody about this just yet.'

She lifted her chin and met his mother's gaze squarely. She didn't want to add to this woman's pain, but she'd do what she could to prevent her from adding to Aidan's. 'It's getting late.'

The dismissal was unmistakable and Vera Fairhall's eyes widened, and then they just as quickly narrowed. 'I will leave the two of you to say your goodnights. Aidan, I expect you in my room—' she gave her room number '—in ten minutes.'

'I really think you ought to leave that till the morning,' Quinn ventured.

The other woman spun to her. 'Don't you dare presume to tell me how to deal with my son!' And then she turned on her eminently respectable court shoe heels and stalked away.

Once she'd disappeared from view, Quinn pulled out of Aidan's grip, lifted both hands and let them drop. 'What on earth did you tell her we were engaged for?'

'I didn't say we were engaged. I said you were the woman I mean to marry.'

'You knew it's what she'd think!'

He scowled. 'She said you were slutty.'

Quinn went back over the conversation. 'No, she didn't.'

'Not just then.' He slashed a hand through the air. 'This morning, when I spoke to her on the phone. She called you my slutty friend.'

Quinn planted her hands on her hips. 'What's wrong with that? It was the look we were aiming for, remember? I'm *supposed* to be the wildly inappropriate woman.'

He stabbed a finger at her. 'She had no right to say it. It seriously cheesed me off.'

That was more than obvious.

'And just now she looked as if you were something unpleasant she'd stepped in.'

'It doesn't matter what she thinks of me.'

'Yes it does!'

Her heart started to pound. She pressed a hand against it. She was *not* going to travel this road with Aidan. 'You're going to have to tell her we're not engaged.'

He thrust out his chin and glowered at her. 'Or you will?'

Not on her life! 'I'll leave that particular joy to you.'

He didn't say anything. Tension crawled in all the spaces and silences between them. 'I'm sorry if this hasn't turned out the way you wanted,' she whispered. She tried to find a smile. 'But you've certainly galvanised your mother to action.' She wanted to reach out and touch him, but the fire burning between them was too fierce and she was afraid of getting burned. 'I just didn't know that it would create so much upheaval in you too.'

He dragged a hand down his face. 'Quinn...?'

She pulled herself up and glanced at her watch. She was *not* inviting him back to her room. 'Please don't lose your temper with her tonight. Try to get out of there as quickly as you can and sleep on it. See how you feel in the morning.'

'Will I see you in the morning?'

'Of course you will.' To say goodbye. She turned and made for the nearest elevator. Aidan didn't follow her and she didn't look back.

Quinn hadn't been in her room fifteen minutes when the phone rang. She grimaced and picked it up. 'Hello?'

'I suspect my mother is on her way to your room.'

Oh, great. Just great. 'You gave her my room number?'

'No, but I know how she operates. She'll have rung down to Reception to get it. Do you want me to come by to intervene?'

Aidan and all of his sexy male temptation in her room? No way! 'I'll deal with it.'

'Are you going to tell her we're not engaged?'

She let out a sigh and she didn't care if he heard it. 'No, but you're going to have to.'

A knock sounded on her door.

'Goodnight, Aidan.'

'A moment of your time, if I may?' Mrs Fairhall said when Quinn opened the door.

She'd have swept into Quinn's room if Quinn hadn't blocked the way. 'On one condition—that you keep your voice down. My boys are sleeping next door and I don't want them disturbed.'

The other woman's eyes flashed, but she nodded and Quinn let her pass.

'You have children?'

'Two boys—eight and six.'

Vera's gaze went to Quinn's left hand.

'And, yes, I'm unmarried. I've also been working in a low-level admin position and I have no tertiary qualifications worth speaking of.'

'That's none of my business.'

'But it's what you came down here to find out.'

She suddenly realised she stood in front of Aidan's mother in an oversized powder-blue T-shirt nightie with the words 'Super Sleep Champion' plastered on the front in big glittery letters. She pulled on the complimentary towelling robe provided for guests and tried not to feel at a disadvantage.

'That's not the reason I came down here, Ms Laverty.'

Quinn gestured to a chair. 'Would you like to sit?'

'I won't be here long enough to bother.'

Quinn sat. She did so in the hope it would help ease the acid burn in her stomach. 'You're here to offer me money to leave Aidan alone.'

'I see you've played this little game before.'

Just the once.

Vera whipped out a chequebook. 'How much will it take?'

And Quinn said now what she'd said back then. 'I don't want your money. I won't accept your money.'

'But—'

'Spare me the arguments. I already know the things I could do with the ludicrous amount of money you'd be prepared to offer me and, yes, I know the advantages my boys could gain from it, but I have too much self-respect. It's more important for me to be able to look my sons in the eye.'

Vera opened her mouth again, but Quinn kept talking right over the top of her. 'I have too much respect for Aidan too. Do you have any idea how furious he'd be if he found out about this?'

Vera fell into the other chair as if she couldn't help it.

'I don't care about the insult offered to me. After all, what are we to each other? But the insult offered to Aidan...' Her hands clenched about the arms of her chair. 'How can you show him such little respect?'

'You will ruin him!' The older woman's face twisted. 'You will ruin everything good that he stands for.'

'How can you give him so little credit?' She sat back, her stomach churning harder and faster. The people from Aidan's world, though, would agree with Vera, would believe what she said with every conceited, supercilious bone in their bodies. They'd believe that a woman like her would blight Aidan's life.

Aidan was from that world, just as Phillip had been, and eventually he'd believe it too. She pulled in a breath. She and Aidan were *not* going to travel down the same path she and Phillip had. She'd make sure of it.

Not that Vera Fairhall knew that. She thought she was fighting for her son's reputation. The only son she had left.

Quinn reached across and squeezed Vera's hand. 'I know of your recent troubles and I'm very sorry for your loss. More sorry than I can say.'

'You know nothing!' Vera pulled her hand away, but she looked as if she might cry.

'You're right. I've never suffered a loss like that. The very thought of it makes me feel ill.'

Vera turned back.

'Aidan has talked to me about it a little. I know he and his father have been very worried about you and that they've been searching for ways to try and help you in your grief.'

'This is none of your business!'

'But in amongst all of this awfulness, who's been looking out for Aidan?'

'Don't you dare!'

Why not? Somebody had to. She leaned towards Vera. 'He's lost a brother he loved more than he's ever loved himself.'

'And you're taking advantage of his grief!'

Vera's pain was almost tangible. Quinn's eyes burned. 'No,' she said as gently as she could. 'I'm not the one who's taking advantage of him.'

Air hissed out from between Vera's teeth.

'If you continue trying to turn him into Danny, Mrs Fairhall, you'll have not only lost one son— you'll have lost the both of them.'

Vera rose and left Quinn's room without another word.

'That went well,' she whispered to the ceiling. And then she flung herself face down on her bed and burst into tears.

Quinn mightn't have slept much, but nevertheless she was up before either Robbie or Chase the next morning. The knock on her door, when it came, didn't surprise her.

Vera or Aidan?

She opened it.

Aidan.

She stood back to let him in and then went to

the window and pushed the curtains even wider, flooding every inch of the room with as much sunlight as she could. It didn't erase the seductive appeal of the queen-sized bed, but it helped. A bit.

'The boys?'

'Still asleep.'

'Right. Okay.' He adjusted his stance. 'There's been a change of plan.'

Her stomach started to pitch and her heart grew heavy. 'Oh?'

'I'm going to accompany you as far as Sydney now.'

She gripped her hands together and shook her head. 'No.'

He frowned. He started to open his mouth.

'You're not invited,' she said before he could speak. 'This was always where we were going to part ways and we're sticking to that original plan.'

He turned grey then and she ached for him. It took all of her strength to remain where she was rather than racing across and flinging her arms around him.

He strode across and thrust a finger beneath her nose. 'We are more than ships in the night, regardless of what you think.' His voice was low and it shook, but there was no mistaking his sincerity.

Maybe. Maybe not. But one thing was certain. 'I will not be used as some kind of distraction or delaying tactic. You need to sort your life out, Aidan. Not tomorrow or next week or after you've lost the campaign, but now. And if you think putting it off is helping anyone then think again.'

He glared. She glared back, but she couldn't maintain it. 'I want to tell you something.' She sat in one of the tub chairs, though fell might've been a more accurate description.

He folded himself into the other. 'Go on.' His voice was so chilly it raised gooseflesh on her arms.

She met his gaze. 'Children don't owe their parents diddly-squat.'

His head rocked back. 'Steady on!'

'If parents inspire respect and love, that's great, but it doesn't mean children owe their parents a damn thing. It's the parents who owe their children.' She leaned towards him to try and drive her point home. 'It's the parents—or parent— who made the decision to bring a child into the world. It's therefore the parents' responsibility to keep that child safe and healthy. It's therefore the parents' responsibility to give that child as good a life as they can.'

'And the good schools and the extracurricular sporting activities and music lessons and the overseas trips, they all count for nothing?'

'Be grateful for them, by all means, but it doesn't mean you owe your mother and father for having provided them for you. And it definitely doesn't mean you have to lead the life they'd like to lock you into. Parents, if they've actually been successful at parenting, should've instilled in their children the strength to choose their own paths.'

'You're calling me weak?'

'I am not! But I think your grief and your worry for your mother has clouded your judgement.'

He leaned towards her and her throat tightened. 'You know what I think? I think this reasoning of yours is flawed, coloured by your experience with your own family.'

She tried not to flinch.

'Do you really think complete self-abnegation and self-sacrifice is a healthy example to give your kids? Do you want them to grow up thinking that finding a job they don't like but that will pay the bills is the best they can hope for out of life?'

Her jaw dropped.

'I don't know what you're scared of, Quinn, by refusing to go to university. Maybe you're afraid that you'll turn into your parents.'

She shot to her feet, shaking. 'That will *never* happen.'

He leapt up too. 'Or maybe it's the fact that some of what they said nine years ago was the truth.'

'They said we'd ruin our lives. I don't consider my life ruined.' Regardless of what Phillip thought to the contrary.

'But it's been no bed of roses.'

Her chin shot up. 'Do you hear me complaining?'

He stared at her for a long moment and then swore softly. 'I'm sorry. I shouldn't have said any of that.'

She rubbed her nose. 'I'm not going to apologise for what I said. I meant every word of it. And I think it needed to be said.'

Aidan tried to tamp down on the fear that rolled through him. This couldn't be goodbye. It *couldn't!*

He shoved his shoulders back. Quinn was running scared and who could blame her? For pity's sake, she was a single mother with more than one life to consider. *And* she'd met his mother.

The world they'd been living in for the last... eight...nine days? It had been a strange, contained and intense time—time out of time was what she'd called it—but that didn't make it any less real.

Everything had changed.

It occurred to him, with a wisdom he'd totally lacked these last few months, that a little time apart could be good for both of them. He needed to think. Hard.

But he wasn't letting her leave without extracting a promise that he could see her again. 'Can I come see you and the boys once you're settled?'

He could see the refusal forming on her lips when Chase burst into the room. He flung his arms around his mother's middle and beamed at Aidan. 'We had fun with Holly last night. Can we stay another day? I love Adelaide!'

Quinn chuckled, a rich warm sound he knew he'd miss. 'I'm sure you do, but today we hit the road again, buster.'

Chase pouted, but his heart wasn't really in

it. And then his face changed completely from fun and mischief to something sombre and glum. 'Are you really not coming with us, Aidan?'

Aidan swore that every muscle Quinn possessed tightened until she practically hummed with tension. Chase had just handed him the perfect tool to worm his way back into their car for the rest of the journey. A glance at Quinn told him it wouldn't win him any Brownie points, though.

He crouched down in front of Chase. 'I'm afraid I have to get back to work, but I've had the best fun hanging out with you guys.'

Chase's bottom lip wobbled. Aidan whipped a business card from his wallet. 'See that number there?' He pointed. 'How about you ring it this evening to tell me where you are and what you did for the day?'

Chase's eyes widened and he was all smiles again. 'Okay!'

Quinn smiled her thanks. A guarded thanks, admittedly, but at the moment he'd take any kind of smile from her that he could get.

He rose to find Robbie surveying them from the doorway—*scowling* from the doorway. 'Hey, buddy.' How long had he been standing there, watching and listening?

Robbie didn't answer. Aidan had learned that Robbie, unlike his brother, wasn't precisely a morning person, but he sensed this was more than a case of the just-out-of-bed grumps.

Robbie glared at his mother.

Aidan pushed his shoulders back. He wasn't having Robbie blaming Quinn for this situation. 'I'm really sorry to abandon ship on you guys, but I have to be back in Sydney today.'

Robbie blinked and he looked so suddenly vulnerable an ache started up in Aidan's chest. 'I know, mate, I'm really going to miss you guys too.'

When Robbie started to cry, he couldn't help himself. He strode across, picked the young boy up and moved across to Quinn's bed. A glance at Quinn and her too-shiny eyes told him she was close to tears too. Chase pressed his face into her side.

'Boys aren't supposed to cry, are they?' Robbie eventually hiccupped, his storm over.

'Of course they are.' Aidan shifted, except... He glanced at Quinn. She wouldn't like it if he told the boys otherwise.

He glanced at each of the boys again. Darn it all! 'Chase, come up here too and I'll let you both in on a little secret.'

Chase raced over and climbed up beside him. Quinn folded her arms. Her eyes narrowed.

'It's always okay to cry with your mum. She's probably the absolute best person in the world to cry with. And I bet your Aunt Mara will be a good person to cry with too.'

'She is,' Robbie confided. 'And so are you.'

It was the strangest compliment he'd ever received, but a stupid smile spread across his face and his chest puffed out.

Chase nudged him. 'What's the secret?'

He sobered. 'It's not fair,' he warned, 'but life will be much easier if you don't cry in front of your friends at school. It's okay for girls, but not so much for boys.'

Chase looked across to Robbie. 'Is that true?'

Robbie bit his lip. 'I think it is, even though everyone says it's not.'

'Aidan!'

Quinn stood with her hands on her hips and her eyes flashing.

He lifted a shoulder. 'Look, I know it's not fair,

but it's true. And I want the boys to have an easy time of it at school.'

Her lovely lips parted and a wave of desire washed over him. He gritted his teeth and searched for a way to soothe ruffled maternal feathers. 'Boys, I think if someone should cry, though, that's okay and that he shouldn't be teased for it.'

Robbie stared up at him.

'So if that ever does happen—' Aidan met Robbie's gaze square on '—I don't think you should join in the teasing. What's more, I think you should stick up for him.'

Robbie scratched his nose. 'That could be hard sometimes,' he finally ventured.

'I know.' Aidan pulled in a breath. 'Doing the right thing often is.'

And so, he was discovering, was parenting. It sure as heck wasn't for the faint-hearted. It wasn't all days at the beach and trips to the zoo. Which reminded him...

He met Quinn's gaze. He hadn't used the opening Chase had given him earlier as leverage, but... Her eyes narrowed, as if sensing he was up to something. Man, she wouldn't like this.

But he wasn't letting her go without a fight.

'Robbie and Chase, remember how I said we should all go to Taronga Park Zoo in Sydney?'

They both nodded vigorously.

'How about we do exactly that this Saturday?' It was Monday today. It'd give Quinn plenty of time to get to Pokolbin—she'd probably be there by Thursday.

Both boys leapt off the bed to jump and cheer. Quinn gaped at them, and at him. 'But...but we just spent a day at a zoo.'

He rose with a grin. 'Boys can never have too much of a zoo, Quinn.'

She pointed a finger at him, her brows darkening. 'You—'

He caught her finger and brought it to his lips. The pulse at the base of her throat throbbed and a deep ravaging hunger shook him. He had to get out of here. 'That evening is my parents' anniversary party. Please say you'll accompany me.'

Her jaw dropped. She hauled it back in place and nibbled at her lip. 'I...'

'We'll hire a couple of motel rooms in the city, just like we have here, and maybe we could do something on the Sunday before you have to head back to Pokolbin.'

'Say yes, Mum,' Robbie breathed.

She tried to tug her hand free, but Aidan refused to release it until he had her answer. She shifted her weight from one foot to the other. 'You were very good with the boys just then.'

He could be very good for her too, if she'd let him.

As if she'd read that thought in his face, her cheeks flamed. Finally she nodded. 'The zoo sounds like fun.'

'The party will be too,' he assured her. Maybe by then he'd have worked out which was the wiser course—to leave Quinn alone or to pursue her with everything he had.

'What do you mean, you don't want a political career after all? You were the one who decided to step into Daniel's shoes!'

This was not going to be an easy conversation, but Quinn had been right—trying to live Danny's life was never going to work. Not for anyone. Not in the long run.

'I will not allow you to let him down like this!' Every perfectly coiffed hair on his mother's head rippled in outrage.

'But it's okay with you if I let myself down?'

She stiffened. She stared and his heart ached and ached for her. He loved his mother. He loved both of his parents. He'd loved Danny too.

And Quinn?

He swallowed. Quinn understood him, she'd fought for him, she was strong and full of laughter and she'd made the sun shine in his miserable life again. He wasn't sure what any of that meant.

Maybe they were only ships in the night, but everything inside him rebelled at that thought.

'Aidan!'

His mother's words snapped him to. He pulled in a breath. First he had to fight for his life—for the life he wanted to lead. He wouldn't deserve Quinn otherwise. 'Dad asked me to take Danny's place.'

She sat, slowly, as if her bones hurt. 'Why?'

Her voice came out hoarse and he had to close his eyes for a moment. 'He thought it would give you a reason to...to keep going.'

Her eyes filled and his chest cramped. 'And I agreed to do it because I love you both and I wanted to do whatever I could to make you feel better and to fill the void Danny had left behind. But I'm not Danny. I'm never going to be Danny. And nothing is ever going to fill that void.'

'So on the strength of that you're going to let Danny's legacy die?'

His head came up. 'Danny's legacy wasn't his political career.' He stared at her for a long moment and then said, 'Do you know how long it's been since I went surfing?'

She waved an impatient hand. 'Grow up, Aidan. We all put away childish things.'

'Danny didn't.'

'Of course he did! He—'

'He attended every single home game the Swans had last year,' he said, naming one of the premier football teams in the country. 'He had a box.' Aidan found himself grinning. 'He told you and Dad it was for networking and hobnobbing, but it was really because he loved his footy.'

His mother gaped at him. He lowered himself down to the seat beside her. 'Danny's legacy wasn't his career, Mum. It was his love of life and how he managed to instil that into everyone he came into contact with. It was his support of my surfing, Dad's golf and your book club. Danny wouldn't want you sitting inside four walls constantly grieving. He'd want you out and about, doing the things you love and sharing that love with others, just as he did.'

She leapt up and wheeled away. 'You think it's easy to move on? You think a person—a mother—can do it just like that?' She snapped her fingers.

'I know it's not easy.' He rested his forehead against his palm and drew in a breath that made him shudder. If he continued to pursue Quinn it would cause his mother yet more grief. Could he really do that to her at the present time? 'I realise I'm not your firstborn, and I know I'm not your favourite son, but—'

She spun around. 'Your father and I didn't have favourites!'

Aidan lifted his chin. 'Danny was everything you wanted in a son. He was your golden boy. Mum, I don't mean to sound harsh, I loved Danny, but his life is not worth more than mine.'

She sat as if in a dream. She reached out as if to touch him, but drew back at the last moment. 'I didn't realise that's how you felt. Why have you never told me this before?'

He shrugged.

Her eyes flashed. Her hair quivered. 'You stupid boy! You should've said something!'

He blinked.

'That rotten reserve of yours, Aidan! Danny was always effusive and affectionate. It was very easy to show him affection in return and to be demonstrative with him. It was always much harder to break through your reserve.'

His jaw dropped.

'I can see why you might think we favoured Danny, but, son, that just wasn't the case.'

It wasn't? He'd spent all this time thinking he was the second son in every sense and yet...

'Come along, Aidan, it's time for us to catch a plane and head into this brave new world of ours.'

He caught hold of her hand. 'I've had a thought about our brave new world. Mum, you're as passionate about politics as Dad and Danny ever were. Why don't you stand for office?'

'Me? But that's nonsense!'

'Why? You're only fifty-three, and an energetic fifty-three at that. You know the ropes. You know how to play the game. You'd be an absolute asset to the party.'

Her jaw dropped but he could see her mind ticking over as his idea took hold.

'I'll go and pack.' Aidan rose, and he left with a lighter heart than he could've thought possible.

CHAPTER NINE

THE MOMENT THE knock sounded on Quinn's motel room door the following Saturday evening, a tempest burst to life in her stomach. The knock wasn't loud—a firm unhurried rat-tat—but it was clear and distinct. It *wasn't* enough to send a stampede of a thousand thrashing wings thumping through her.

At least, it shouldn't have been.

She pressed a hand to her stomach, moistened her lips and eased the door open, fighting the urge to fling it wide to feast her eyes on the man who stood on its other side. She'd already feasted her eyes on him earlier in the day when she'd found him waiting for her and the boys at the entrance to Taronga Park Zoo.

He'd feasted his eyes on her then too—just as hungrily, just as intensely, and with an intent that had made her stomach tighten.

The boys hadn't considered hiding their excitement. They'd hurled themselves at him, talking ten to the dozen. She'd envied them their lack of restraint. She'd have loved to have hugged him, but she hadn't. She'd merely nodded. He'd given her a quick peck on the cheek and his scent had filled her with so much longing it was all she'd been able to do to not run away.

Robbie and Chase had had the most brilliant day.

She hadn't. And she hadn't been able to tell if Aidan had or not either. She'd tried to take pleasure in the boys' joy, in the gorgeous views of Sydney Harbour and in the antics of the meerkats, but her awareness of Aidan drove everything else out of her. That awareness had grown as the day progressed—a deep prickling burn that wore away at her. Conversation didn't ease it. At least, not the kind of polite surface chit-chat they'd maintained.

She gritted her teeth. They'd maintain it this evening too if it killed her. And then they'd never see each other again and she'd be free to get on with her life. Whatever sense of obligation had prompted Aidan would be allayed.

The thought made her want to throw up.

It also made her want to heave a sigh of relief.

He frowned. 'Are you feeling all right?'

She snapped a smile to her face. 'Of course.'

He stared at her. She stared back. Okay, polite chit-chat *but* with a little drop of honesty thrown in. 'Are you sure you'd still like me to accompany you this evening?'

'Why would you ask me that?'

His voice came out deceptively soft. It raised gooseflesh on her arms. She tried to rub it away. 'Aidan, this is a party to honour your parents. I imagine your mother, and probably your father too, will be far from thrilled that I'm attending as your date.'

'You leave my parents to me.'

Gladly, but would they return the favour? Or would she be trotted off to some quiet alcove and offered some other sweetie to disappear into the night and never return?

'I won't be offended if you've changed your mind.'

The aggressive tilt to his chin made her mouth water. 'I will be if you've changed yours.'

She bit back a sigh. 'Fine, okay. So be it.' She collected her wrap and purse. 'I guess we'd best set off. We don't want to be late.'

'Are you determined to treat this entire evening like an unpleasant chore?'

That pulled her up short. 'Of course not!' But it was true. She expected this evening to be an ordeal. Which was hardly fair to Aidan. 'I'm just concerned that…' She'd ruin everything for him.

'Well, don't be.' He took her wrap—a shot silk stole that matched her dress—and settled it around her shoulders. 'By the way, you look lovely.'

His breath disturbed the hair by her ear and sent a shiver arrowing down to pulse at a spot below her belly button. 'Thank you.' Her voice wobbled, betraying her.

His grip on her shoulders tightened and he pulled her back against him to show her how much she affected him too. Her breath caught. She closed her eyes, but rather than help her regain her balance it only highlighted the hardness pressing against her.

'If this were any other night I would do my best to seduce you here and now.'

She wasn't sure she'd have the strength to resist him if he did. With a superhuman effort she moved out of his grasp. 'But it isn't any other night. Besides, you look very debonair in your dinner jacket and black tie and it would be a shame to wrinkle you.' She could just imagine his mother's face!

She turned. 'I left the vamp behind tonight to dress as a lady. It's how I expect to be treated.'

He stared back at her, his eyes darker than she'd ever seen them. The very air throbbed. 'Have I ever treated you as anything else?'

'No.' He hadn't.

'C'mon, let's go.'

He took her elbow. She had to grit her teeth and lecture herself long and hard to keep her inner vamp under wraps.

The party was held in the ballroom of one of the city's grand hotels. It had glorious views of the Harbour and the Opera House. Lights twinkled on the Harbour and fairy lights winked on the two hundred guests—the elite of Sydney society—who mingled in all of their glamorous finery, and Quinn wished herself back into the isolation of the Nullarbor Plain and a night sky filled with an entirely different kind of light show.

She'd known Aidan would have hosting duties this evening. She'd known he would have to leave her for long periods of time. She hadn't minded. He'd introduced her to nice people. She'd made pleasant conversation. And it had given her a chance to observe him without his knowing.

'I understand you and my son had quite the adventure.'

Quinn swung from surveying the Harbour to find Aidan's father holding out a glass of champagne to her. She took it—without a single shake or quiver and all while maintaining a smile. Well done her! 'Happy anniversary, Mr Fairhall.' She touched her glass lightly to his. They both sipped. 'An adventure?' she finally said. 'Yes, I guess it was.'

Mr Fairhall opened his mouth, but his wife chose that moment to glide up between them. 'You look lovely this evening, Quinn. That dress is quite charming.'

She and her aunt had spent an entire day searching for this dress. She'd told Mara everything, of course. Mara had chuckled and decreed that Quinn needed a dress fit for a lady—a dress fit for Audrey Hepburn. And they'd found it. Pink silk shot through with the merest shimmer of black. Cocktail length with a scalloped hem, embroidered in black and with matching embroidery on the bodice. It was pretty, demure and very, *very* chic.

Quinn, however, caught the underlying meaning to Vera Fairhall's words. 'Thank you, Mrs Fairhall. The dress cost a bomb, but it was worth every penny.' She named the designer and had the satisfaction of seeing Vera's eyes widen. 'But we both know clothes don't make the woman.'

'That is very true, my dear.' She raised an eyebrow. 'I hear you've had quite the day of it.'

Had Aidan told her about their trip to the zoo? Or did she have spies? And, either way, did it matter? 'Yes, indeed.'

'I certainly understand if you're feeling tired and would like to sneak away early to go and check on your children. I mean we can't spare Aidan, of course, but we'd be more than happy to cover a taxi for you.'

'I'm sure you would,' Quinn said drily. 'Your reputation for hospitality precedes you.'

Tom Fairhall chuckled. Vera drew back. 'I'm only trying to be polite, Quinn. I'd understand if you felt slightly out of place here this evening.'

'Vera,' Tom chided softly.

'Not in the least,' Quinn sent back with all the fake sincerity she could muster. 'I see you even invited my parents. I do hope you didn't do that on my account.'

She gestured across the room. Vera swung to stare and her jaw dropped. 'You're *that* Laverty girl?'

Quinn raised an eyebrow, but her stomach sank. 'You don't need to concern yourself with me, Mrs Fairhall. I won't be troubling you for a taxi. I have a strong constitution and I don't tire easily.'

Vera stalked off. Tom patted Quinn's shoulder. 'Don't mind my wife, my dear. She's always been far too protective of Aidan. It's just become worse since...'

She glanced up uncertainly. 'I understand that. I...' She bit her lip. 'I did say to Aidan it might be best if I didn't come this evening.'

'My son, however, can be very persuasive.'

She smiled at that. 'Still, I don't want to ruin your or your wife's enjoyment of the evening and if you think it's best I leave, I will.'

He stared down at her. He had eyes disarmingly like his son's. 'That's very generous of you, Quinn, but no. While Vera can't see it yet, we owe you a huge debt of gratitude. I'd unknowingly pushed Aidan into a course of action that was wrong for him and I didn't know how to reverse it. You helped him do that instead.'

So Aidan had stood up for himself? He'd turned his back on a political career? Her heart lifted. 'I'm not sure I can take too much credit.'

'I'm sure you're being far too modest.'

She recognised the guilt behind the dark amber of his eyes. 'I don't think you should feel guilty about pointing Aidan towards politics. Grief is a process. I think it helped Aidan more than hindered him.'

He smiled then. 'Thank you, my dear.'

Her parents glanced in her direction, pushed their shoulders back and she read the resolution in their faces. 'Now, off with you,' she shooed, not wanting him to witness whatever was about to transpire. 'You've neglected your guests for long enough.'

With a chuckle he strolled off.

She'd noticed her parents the moment they'd walked into the party—her father in an impeccable suit and her mother in sensible shoes. She wasn't sure how long it had taken them to recognise her. She suspected a percentage of the room was abuzz with news of Aidan's unsuitable girlfriend. Her name would've been passed from group to group and her parents would've heard it.

Not that she was Aidan's girlfriend.

You'd like to be.

It'd never work.

'If you have any sense of shame whatsoever,' her father said without preamble, 'you will leave this party at once.'

She and shame, at least her father's version of it, had never been close acquaintances. She pasted a big fake smile to her face. 'Hello, Daddy, lovely to see you too! You and Mummy look well. I'm sure you'll be delighted to hear that your grand-children are healthy and happy.'

'Don't embarrass us in front of all these people, Quinn,' her mother snapped.

Quinn stared at them and shook her head. She hadn't seen them in nine years. It seemed strange to feel so removed from two people who had once been so important to her. But it was a relief too. She couldn't believe that once upon a time she'd wanted to be just like them.

'So you have your sights set on the Fairhall boy now, taking advantage of a family's grief, deter-mined to ruin yet another man?'

She lifted her chin. 'The two of you lost any

right to have a say in my life when you disowned me nine years ago. You are horrible people who lead sterile lives and I really don't want anything to do with either one of you.'

She'd have told them to go away, but Aidan chose that moment to return to her side. He glanced from her to her parents and back again. 'Quinn?'

'Aidan, these are my parents, Ryan and Wendy Laverty.'

She didn't say 'I'd like you to meet my parents', because that would've been a lie.

She recognised the shock deep in his eyes. Perhaps she should've been a bit more forthcoming about her background on that long drive from Perth, but it had all seemed so separate from her. 'My father is a vice chancellor at a nearby university and my mother is a leading researcher at another.' She gestured to Aidan. 'I expect you both recognise Aidan Fairhall.'

They all shook hands, but nobody smiled. It didn't surprise her when her father was the first to break the silence. 'Young man, I hope you'll take my advice and steer clear of this woman.'

Beside her, Aidan stiffened.

'I assure you that she is nothing but trouble and will only bring you grief.'

'I'm afraid, sir, that I have to disagree with you. Quinn is a remarkable woman with more integrity and true kindness than anyone I've ever met.'

Man, he was good. Smooth, unflappable and unfailingly pleasant.

'And if you say one more disagreeable thing about her I will have to ask you to leave.'

He managed to maintain his smile the entire time. She wanted to applaud.

He turned to Quinn, effectively dismissing her parents. 'Your drink is warm. Let's go get you a fresh one.'

And, with that, he took her elbow and whisked her off to the bar. She slid onto a stool as Aidan ordered their drinks, and when he handed her a mineral water she started to laugh. 'That was masterfully handled.'

'Jeez.' He settled on the stool beside her. 'And I thought my mother was a nightmare.'

Quinn grinned. 'She is.'

He choked on his drink.

She nudged his shoulder. 'I want more for you than a woman who has been around the blocks a few times.'

He winced. 'You heard that?'

'Uh-huh.' As she'd no doubt been meant to. It had been said much earlier in the evening. There'd been some mention of all the baggage Quinn carried too. She'd taken that to refer to Robbie and Chase. When Aidan had turned back to her she'd pretended to be absorbed in studying the table decorations to save him from embarrassment.

But he'd just witnessed her embarrassment.

Was an embarrassment shared an embarrassment halved? She grimaced and sipped her drink. She suspected it might in fact be an embarrassment doubled.

'I'm sorry, Quinn. My mother—'

'Aidan, we put on one heck of a show in Adelaide. Your mother has every right to her reservations. She only has your best interests at heart.'

'Your parents don't, though.' He reached out to squeeze her hand. 'I didn't know they'd be here this evening.'

She squeezed it back before releasing it on the pretext of lifting her drink. The less she and Aidan touched the better. 'Neither did I. I'm sorry if they came as a shock to you. I probably should've been more candid about my background, but...' She glanced up at him. 'It all feels so remote from who I am now.'

Something burned in the backs of his eyes. 'We can leave if you want to.'

'Absolutely not.'

'I'm not buying into this casual nonchalance for a moment, sweetheart.'

Tears burned the backs of her eyes. She forced her chin up. 'But I do have my pride. I have absolutely no intention of giving either your mother or my parents that kind of satisfaction.'

He swore so softly she hardly heard it.

She sent him a smile. 'Besides, I promised your father I'd be one of the last to leave.'

He smiled then too. 'Wanna dance?'

She slid off her stool. 'I thought you'd never ask.'

Aidan walked Quinn to her hotel room. Neither one of them spoke. He didn't touch fingers to her elbow on the pretext of guiding her. He didn't take her hand. He didn't touch the small of her back. He kept his hands firmly—and deeply— in his pockets, did what he could to control the rapid pounding of his heart and reminded himself to keep breathing.

One foot after the other

One breath after the other.

He could do this. His hands clenched. *He could do this.*

They reached her door. They both stared at it for two beats rather than at each other. Finally Quinn seemed to give herself a mental kick and fumbled in her purse for the plastic key card.

He took it from her, inserted it into its slot and pushed the door open a crack. Quinn stared up at him, her eyes wide and uncertain, her lips a tempting promise in the dimly lit corridor.

You can do this!

He didn't step any closer. He would lose all pretence of control if he did that, if all of her sweetness pressed up warm and inviting against him.

Still, he couldn't resist dipping his head to kiss her.

Her lips met his, hesitant perhaps, but undeniably awake to the consequences that could ensue.

She kissed him back as if inviting those consequences. More than anything, he wanted to back her into her room and kiss her until they were both mindless with need. He ached to peel her clothes from her body and explore every inch of her to find what would make her gasp, what would make her moan, what would make her call out his name. He wanted to make love with her, frantic and fast. He wanted to make love with her painstakingly slow. He wanted to lose himself in the mindless pleasure they could find with each other.

But he couldn't let that happen.

He wanted more than one night with this woman. That had come to him swift and sure as he'd watched her make polite conversation with perfect strangers tonight. Quinn mightn't have wanted to attend the party, but not a soul would've guessed it. Meeting her parents had sealed the deal. Despite the pain it would cause his mother, he wanted to keep Quinn in his life.

Although she didn't know it, she held his heart in her hands. One misstep from him and she would drop it cold. And instinct warned him his heart wouldn't bounce. It would take a long time to get over her and he didn't want to have to try.

He deepened the kiss, wanting her aching so hard for him that she couldn't turn and just walk away. She tasted of champagne and coffee. She fizzed in his blood until he felt as if he were riding the biggest, most perfect wave of his life. Bracing one hand against the wall, he sucked her bottom lip into his mouth, nibbled it, laved it with his tongue. Her hands flattened against his chest and started to inch up towards his shoulders. Her tongue tangled with his and she made a mewling noise that angled straight down to his groin.

He broke free. 'Thank you for coming to the party with me this evening.' He didn't try to hide the hoarseness of his voice.

'Aidan?' Her hands slid against his chest and she made no move to hide the glitter in her eyes or the need in her face.

He backed up a step. Her hands fell to her sides. Her eyes dimmed. Disappointment flared in their depths...and relief. The relief kept him strong. Until she wanted him as unreservedly and unashamedly as he wanted her, he wouldn't let things go any further.

He could do this!

'I'll collect you and the boys at ten in the morning.'

'But...' She opened the door wider in silent invitation.

He shook his head. 'Goodnight, Quinn.'

He turned and walked away. He shoved his hands into his pockets and clenched them. He gritted his teeth and placed one foot in front of the other, pulled in one breath after the other.

They spent the following day on the Harbour. Aidan had booked a lunch cruise—family friendly—and he couldn't have ordered more perfect weather. The sun shone, but not too fiercely. A fresh breeze played through their hair, caressing their skin in a way that made it hard for him to think of anything but Quinn naked and his fingers trailing across her flesh. And hers trailing across his.

A burst of laughter from the children on the deck below snapped him back to himself. The colour on Quinn's cheekbones had grown high and he knew she'd read the direction his thoughts had taken. And if the pulse pounding at the base of her throat was any indication, she might have in fact added her own embellishments to the fantasy. His groin started to throb in time to the beat of her pulse.

'Why didn't you stay last night?' The words shot out of her as if some resistance had been breached. They sat alone at a table overlooking the foredeck, but she kept her voice low.

He leaned towards her and he didn't try to temper his intensity. 'Because I want you to want me with the same fire I want you.'

Her lips parted. She swallowed and her tongue snaked out to moisten them. 'Do you doubt it?'

He forced himself back in his seat. 'Are you telling me you didn't feel a thread of relief when I walked away last night?'

She glanced away. It was all the answer he needed.

'Aidan, neither one of us needs this kind of complication in our lives at the moment.'

He took a sip of his soda, but his eyes never left hers. 'Here's a newsflash for you, Quinn, but I don't consider you a complication.'

Her arched eyebrows told him what she thought about that. It might've made him smile a week ago.

'I like your father.'

He let her change the subject. 'I do too.' She laughed, as he'd hoped she would. He wanted to banish those lines of strain around her mouth forever. 'He likes you too.'

She glanced at him and quickly glanced away again. She tucked her hair behind her ears. 'He said you're making the break from politics.'

Thanks to her, he'd found the courage to be honest—to himself and to his family. 'Yes.'

'How's that working out for you all?'

'Very well so far. I'm taking some time off to sort out where I want to go from here, while my mother is still going into the office to sort out everyone else. My father watches us both indulgently from the sidelines and tries to fit in as many games of golf as he can.'

She grinned—one of those loving life grins that could transport him to a better place. 'That's excellent news.'

He reached out and ran a finger across the back of her hand. 'Can we talk about your parents for a moment?'

Her hand clenched and then she moved it out of his reach. 'If you want.' Her words came out reluctantly and his heart burned for her. 'But if you're thinking there's a chance for any kind of reconciliation, I'd counsel you to think again.'

He ached to hug her. 'Unfortunately, sweetheart, I agree with you.'

She blinked. Though whether at his words or the endearment, he had no way of knowing.

'Until they realise they're the ones who should be asking your forgiveness rather than the other way around, they're lost causes as far as I'm concerned.'

Her eyes filled and something snagged deep in his chest. This woman deserved so much more. She deserved to be loved and cherished.

And occasionally challenged.

'That's not going to happen. They have very rigid views about life and how it should be lived and anyone living outside of that box is given a wide berth. It's as if they're afraid it will pollute their ambition.' She drew a smiley face in the condensation of her glass. 'Their status at their universities and within their research communities is what matters to them. It's how they measure their success and happiness. They love their jobs and their institutions.' She scrubbed out the smiley face. 'What they haven't realised yet is that jobs and institutions can't love you back.'

Her parents lived in a rigid, narrow-minded world. The same world he'd been in danger of locking himself into.

'What was it like growing up with them?'

'Oh, I had all the privileges any girl could want.'

'It's not what I asked, Quinn.'

She glanced down at her hands. 'Lonely,' she

finally said. 'It was lonely. My parents worked long, hard hours and when they were home their favourite thing to do in the evenings was work some more.'

He swallowed back the acid that burned his throat. When he'd been growing up his father had had to put in the hard yards, but it hadn't stopped either of his parents from finding time for him and Daniel. And he couldn't forget that for all of his childhood he'd had Danny as a playmate and companion too.

'So when Phillip and I started dating I fell hard. So did he.' She shrugged. 'For a while.'

He understood that completely, but...

'C'mon, out with it.'

He grimaced. It was lucky he had a poker face in the courtroom because it was obvious he didn't have one around Quinn. He drummed his fingers against the table. 'Look, I understand your resentment towards your parents.'

'Resentment?' She shifted. 'Oh, Aidan, so much of that is just water under the bridge. All I want to do now is protect my kids from that kind of influence.'

'By turning your back on a whole way of life?' She frowned.

'It's why you've shunned university, isn't it?'

Her eyes flashed. 'That was *their* dream, not mine. I'm living my dream.'

But she wasn't, was she? The childhood sweetheart was no longer at her side, helping her to negotiate parenthood's tricky waters or sharing love and laughter and all of those other things that made life worth living.

He wanted all those things for her. He wanted to share all of those things with her.

'And, quite frankly, I don't know why you have to keep rabbiting on about it.'

'Because, in a way, you're in danger of becoming just as narrow-minded as your parents.'

She gaped at him. 'I can't believe you just said that.'

Nor he. He had to be crazy. This was no way to woo a woman. But in his heart he knew he was right. Until Quinn fought to lead the life she wanted—the life she deserved—she'd never be truly free to love him. And he wanted her to love him. He wanted that with everything good he had inside him.

'Shunning university and a chance for a better life; is that a way of punishing your parents? Or do you believe that if you reject everything your parents value that you're giving validity to your current life?'

In a twisted way he could see how that might make sense.

'Oh, for heaven's sake!' she snapped. 'I'm not eighteen any more. I know that not everyone who has a degree is as inflexible or as detached as my parents...or as selfish as Phillip.'

She did? Then why wouldn't she even consider exploring her passion for science further?

She leaned towards him. 'You really want to know why I haven't considered furthering my education? It's because I don't want my children growing up lonely like I did.'

He saw then, in a light all too clear and blinding, the full effect her lonely childhood had had upon her. 'Oh, sweetheart.'

'Don't you *Oh, sweetheart*, me.' She batted his hand away. 'You don't understand how many hours I put into my schoolwork. It was something intelligent I could discuss with my parents.' She gave a harsh laugh. 'Oh, they trained me well. Those were the only times when I had their full attention and approval. And nobody could accuse me of being a slow learner. It got that I studied almost obsessively just so I could get a pat on the back from one or other of them.'

She'd learned to throw herself into her studies in the same way her parents had thrown themselves into their careers.

'My boys deserve to have a mother who is fully focused on them, not poring over some dusty old tomes in the library during their soccer games and forgetting parent and teacher evenings.'

He finally caught hold of the hand that had been making agitated circles in the air. 'Quinn, honey, you already have more life experience than either of your parents. You haven't been constrained by the narrowness of their world for nine years. You just told me you're not eighteen any more. And you're not. Nor are you going to turn into your parents. Ever. Regardless of whatever else you decide to do with your life.'

She stilled. Beneath his fingertips, her pulse pounded like wild surf.

'Quinn, these days your life is full and rich. It's better than the kind of life you'd be leading if you'd followed your parents' path, yes?'

'Of course.'

'You no longer need to find something that will plug up the loneliness, do you?'

She shook her head.

'Then why don't you believe that you can re-invent your old dreams into the life you're living now? Why don't you trust yourself to make it work?'

She stared at him as if in a daze, as if what he was proposing had never occurred to her before.

'For some reason, your parents couldn't manage to be good scientists and good parents. Phillip hasn't been able to manage that leap either. But you're better than all of them. If you want to, you *can* make it work.'

Her chin came up. He wondered if she realised how tightly she gripped his hand. 'What makes you so sure?'

'Your love for your sons.'

She bit her lip.

He squeezed her hand and then he released it. 'You showed me I had to fight to live the life I was meant to be leading. You showed me I had the right to that life. Exactly the same goes for you.'

CHAPTER TEN

QUINN GLANCED UP from the kitchen table when she heard a car pull in behind the house. Aunt Mara's sturdy farmhouse was set well back from the lane, hidden in among the olive groves like a house in a fairy tale. The driveway was marked 'Private' so it was rare for tourists to accidentally wander down this way, though it did happen.

Mara had left for the shop over an hour ago. Quinn had manned the shop yesterday so today she and the boys were having a traditional lazy Sunday morning. She marked her spot in the university prospectus and moved to peer out of the door, ready to offer directions to whoever might be lost.

A man unfolded himself from the car. She blinked. What on earth...? Aidan!

Her heart hammered up into her throat, making her head whirl. She clung to the doorframe, unable to drag her gaze from the long clean lines of an athletic male body that filled her with a vigour and energy completely at odds with lazy Sundays.

After last weekend she hadn't thought she would see him again. She'd spent a ludicrous amount of time during this last week silently detailing all the reasons why that was a good thing. Absurdly, all she wanted to do now was jump up and down and clap her hands. Which was exactly what Robbie and Chase did when they caught sight of him from where they played in the side yard.

They bolted up to him and he hugged them both as if it were the most natural thing in the world. He grinned as if he were truly delighted to see them. And then he glanced to where she stood and he grinned as if he were truly delighted to see her too and her stomach twisted and turned like a purring cat weaving around its beloved owner's legs. Before she was even aware of it, she was across the veranda and down the back steps. 'Aidan, what a surprise.'

He bent to kiss her cheek. 'Not an unwelcome one, I hope.'

His scent and the touch of his lips woke her up more effectively than a strong shot of espresso. 'Of course not.'

'We can show Aidan everything!' Robbie said.

Aidan took them all in with one comprehensive glance...and that oh-so-beguiling smile of his. 'So you're all still enjoying your new home?'

He had a way of asking a question that made it seem as if he really cared about the answer. Both boys nodded vigorously.

'You can meet Auntie Mara and see the shop!' Chase said.

Chase had fallen under the spell of both, to Quinn's delight.

'And we'll take you down to the dam. We've got ducks!' Robbie added. 'And then we'll show you all the olive trees and—'

'Boys,' she hollered over the top of them when they both started to shout out their plans, 'let Aidan catch his breath first. You must've left at the crack of dawn to get here by ten.'

One shoulder lifted. A lean, broad shoulder that made her mouth water. 'I'm an early riser.'

She shook herself. 'Coffee?'

'Love one.'

It wasn't until they were seated with their coffees that the urge to run hit Quinn. She couldn't explain it. It might've been the way those clear amber eyes surveyed her. It might've been the way they widened when they registered the university prospectus sitting on the table. It might've been the way his presence seemed to fill the kitchen. Whatever it was, it had her wanting to back up and run for the hills. Of course her inner vamp called her an idiot and dared her to sit on his lap instead. The idea left her squirming in her seat.

'Are you here for the whole day?' Robbie demanded.

'If that's okay with your mother.'

Three sets of eyes swung to her. 'I...' She swallowed. Why was he here?

He sent her a winning smile. 'I've heard so much about the place that curiosity got the better of me. I had to see it with my own eyes.'

'We can show you our new school too,' Robbie said.

'And where my friend Andrew lives,' Chase said.

'And the olive presses!'

'And—'

'Boys!' She clapped her hands. 'You're going to give Aidan half an hour to catch his breath after his long drive, while I make him something to eat.'

'Aw, but—'

'No buts.' She shooed them outside. 'You can make up an itinerary for the day.'

Robbie's face lit up and he grabbed Chase's arm. 'Will we start with the dam or the shop?'

She turned back. 'Eggs on toast?'

'I couldn't possibly put you out like that.'

'It's not putting me out at all.' It'd give her something to do, other than sit at the table and stare at him. 'Scrambled okay?'

'Perfect.'

She busied herself with breaking eggs into a bowl.

'It's not that far, you know?'

She glanced across at him. 'What isn't?'

'The drive from Sydney. It's two hours of mostly good road.'

'Oh.' She didn't know what else to say and the silence started to grow. She tried to focus on not burning anything—the eggs, the toast or herself. Eventually she slid a plate of scrambled egg and toast in front of him and hoped it'd ease the itch that had settled squarely between her shoulder blades.

The smile he sent her and his, 'This looks great,' only made her itch worse.

And the silence continued to grow.

'You were right,' she suddenly blurted out, slapping a hand down on the prospectus.

'I wasn't going to ask. I figured I'd hassled you enough. But I've been sitting here dying of curiosity.'

He grinned. She absolutely, positively couldn't help it. She had to grin back. He paused mid-bite to stare and those amber eyes of his darkened. Her heart stopped. Heat scorched her cheeks. She dragged the prospectus towards her and tried to focus beyond the buzz in her brain.

'Food technology is incredibly interesting,' she babbled. 'And can you believe it? Here I am, living on an *olive farm* and the processing of the olives is far more complicated than I ever thought it could be. Not only that, but there's the potential for us to expand our operations from providing just table olives. We could make our own olive oil too. And, I mean…' She knew she was jabbering, but couldn't help it. 'Obviously, that's down the track a bit, but…' She shrugged and forced herself to stop.

'It sounds fascinating.'

She glanced up to see if he was making fun of

her, but sincerity radiated from him. 'You sound as if you've hit the ground running, Quinn, as if you've found your groove.'

'That's exactly what it feels like.'

'I'm happy for you. Really happy.'

She believed him.

He set his knife and fork down and patted his stomach. 'That hit the spot. Thank you.'

She collected up his plate and cutlery. 'I should be the one thanking you. If you hadn't kept hassling me about the possibility of going to uni I'd have continued to dismiss it. You made me shine a light on my own irrationality.' She grimaced, shrugged and tried to scratch the spot that itched. 'I felt that I'd lost my parents and Phillip to higher education. I mean that's utter rubbish, of course. I lost them to their own ambitions and prejudices. And you were right—in pursuing further study I won't become like them. I'll never be like them.'

'I'm glad you can see that now.'

She wouldn't have if it hadn't been for him. The sense of obligation weighed heavily on her, though, and she didn't know why. She rinsed his plate. 'I can't believe how many different study options there are. I have the choice of full-time, part-time, distance and all sorts of mixed mode delivery methods.' It made it very easy for people like her to fit study in around a busy timetable.

But enough about her. 'How are things in Sydney?'

'Excellent! I'm doing some freelance work for my old law firm.'

His grin told her how much he was enjoying it.

'And the big news is that my mother is running Derek Oxford's campaign.'

She did her best to pick her jaw up off the floor. 'Derek...your old second in command?'

'The very one.'

She sat. 'Wow! We've created a monster.'

'She's brilliant at it.'

'I don't doubt it for a moment.' She found herself laughing. 'I don't envy the opposition parties at all.'

'Mum, is it time yet?' Robbie and Chase stared from the doorway.

Aidan smiled, his eyes alive with fun. 'Are you up for a day of showing me around your new life, Quinn?'

A thrill shook through her. She leapt up. 'Just give me a few minutes to get ready.'

Quinn raced off to her bedroom with its tiny en-suite bathroom. It wasn't until she'd pulled on one of her prettiest blouses, though, that it suddenly hit her—she'd just put on a full face of make-up and pulled on her best jeans. A slow churning in her stomach had her dropping to the side of her bed. *What on earth do you think you're doing?*

She and Aidan, they weren't going anywhere. Things between them weren't going to progress beyond friendship.

They already have.

Then she had to put a stop to it before it was too late and someone got hurt.

She was not going to dress up for Aidan. She was not going to try and look pretty for him. She was not going to flirt with him. He might not consider her a complication yet, but he would eventually and she wasn't *ever* going to let that opportunity arise.

Slowly she stowed her pretty blouse back into the wardrobe and then went to scrub her face clean. She slipped on a long-sleeved button-down shirt that covered her from neck to mid-thigh. It was respectable, boring and asexual.

She glanced in the mirror and grimaced. Perfect.

* * *

Even though Quinn did her very best to maintain her guard, she had a day filled with laughter and fun. Aidan even taught them all a new fun novelty song.

'You've chosen a spectacularly beautiful place to live,' he said.

'I can't believe how beautiful it is here,' she admitted. Pokolbin was Hunter Valley wine country. Vineyards and grapevines spilled across gently rolling hills that spread out lazily in every direction. The vistas that greeted her whenever she topped a rise could still make her catch her breath. 'I never realised I was such a rural girl at heart.'

'Aidan, I have a problem,' Robbie suddenly said, his face serious and his eyes puckered.

They'd stopped for cake and coffee—milkshakes for the boys—and his young face looked so serious she straightened on her seat. He hadn't mentioned anything to her!

'What's up, buddy?'

Aidan took her son's words completely in his stride. She rolled her shoulders and forced herself to sit back in her chair.

'I don't like olives,' he whispered. 'And Chase doesn't either.'

She had to bite her lip to hide a smile, her heart filling with love for her serious elder son.

'We don't like olives, but Aunt Mara and...' he shot her a glance '... Mum love them. And I know that they're the reason we live out here and that we have money for food and other stuff. And we love living out here, but...they taste awful!'

'I see,' Aidan said, just as serious as her son.

Robbie crumbled off a piece of his cake. 'It makes me feel bad that I don't like them.'

She opened her mouth, but a swift glance from Aidan had her shutting it again.

'It's not that you don't like olives, guys. It's just that you don't like the taste of them. And, frankly, mostly it's adults who like to eat olives anyway so I don't think you should feel bad.' He leaned in closer. 'You know what you could say?'

Both boys stared at him. He had their complete attention and her eyes suddenly burned. They hungered for a male influence in their lives. Problem was, it was the one thing she couldn't give them.

'You can say that you love olives, but you just

don't like to eat them. And by not eating any that leaves the farm all the more to sell.'

Robbie's face lit up. 'And that means more money for the farm!'

'Precisely.'

With both boys happy again, Aidan winked at her over the rim of his mug and she realised she had to put a stop to all of this as soon as she could. When she'd been worried, earlier, about someone getting hurt. She'd been thinking about him. She'd been thinking about herself. Not her boys. With each visit he won a little more of their trust and was given another piece of their hearts.

Her mouth dried. What had she been thinking? She couldn't risk their happiness like that.

She glanced down into her mug. She hadn't been thinking. That was the problem. She'd been too busy enjoying the ride, enjoying feeling like a desirable woman again, which just went to show what a fool she was.

'Are you okay?'

She glanced up to find those amber eyes focused on her. They narrowed to slits at whatever they saw in her face. He glanced at his watch and then slapped a hand to the table. 'Eat up, guys.

It's almost time we were back at the shop like we promised your aunt.'

Mara had conscripted the boys into helping for the last hour this afternoon. It had been her way of tactfully ensuring that Quinn and Aidan had some time alone. Luckily, the boys loved helping in the shop. At the time Quinn had gritted her teeth at these machinations, but now she was grateful for them.

The sooner she brought a halt to all of this, the better.

Her heart slumped. So did her shoulders. There was nothing she could do about her heart, but she forced her shoulders back, forced a smile to her face. 'My cake was delicious. How was yours?'

It occurred to her then that it'd be a long time before she could face a piece of cake again with any equanimity.

'You want to tell me what's wrong?'

Quinn and Aidan strolled among the olive trees, back towards the house after having walked the boys to the on-site shop. The Olive Branch was a small but charming sandstone building stocked with olives picked from Mara's olive groves along with sourdough bread sourced from a local bakery, cheese from a local cheese maker and an assortment of recipe books.

Tourists found the place irresistible. To be perfectly frank, so did she and the boys. She and Aidan had stayed to watch the boys serve several customers and the way their chests had puffed out at Aidan's praise had made her heart burn.

'Quinn?'

Oh, how to do this gently?

She turned and swallowed. 'Aidan, I really like you. You're a lovely man.'

He closed his eyes and swore. Her heart clenched up harder and smaller than an olive stone.

'Give us some time, Quinn, please, before launching us into this kind of conversation.'

He opened his eyes and they flamed at her.

'Why?' she croaked. 'What would be the point?'

'The point?' He straightened. He shifted his stance, as if trying to hold back a torrent of angry words. Beyond him, the sun had started to lower behind the ridge of the ranges, turning the day smoky even as the edges of everything somehow retained their clarity. She glanced around at all the golden greenness and blue afternoon beauty and wondered how despair could eat away at her so completely.

This morning she'd been happy!

This morning you were still hiding your head in the sand.

He leaned towards her, his jaw set. 'The point is we have the chance to develop something not just good but spectacular if you give us a chance.'

Her heart pounded and her every muscle twitched. If she'd been a bird she'd have taken flight. Even thinking about what he proposed hurt. Hoping for what could never be hurt.

You ruined my life! She would never give Aidan the chance to hurl those words at her.

'You're wrong.' She might be crumbling inside but her voice emerged strong and sure. 'You have to stop coming around. The boys are coming to love you too dearly. They're starting to depend on you too heavily. This has to stop before someone gets hurt.'

His gaze held hers, fierce and strong. 'It's too late for that, Quinn. I'm already in too deep.'

A tremble shook her. She swayed. Whatever golden was left of the day leached out of it. 'Oh, Aidan.'

He stood straight and proud like a warrior and

it occurred to her that he must cut a commanding figure in a courtroom. She might have just dealt his hopes a deathblow, but he was neither cowed nor vanquished.

His chin lifted. 'I can't believe you won't even consider the possibility of us.'

Scorn, closely held in check, rippled beneath his words. She flinched.

'Why?' he demanded. 'Why won't you even consider it?'

She flung an arm out. 'Let me count the ways!'

He widened his stance and folded his arms. 'Then let's have them.'

The amber of his eyes glowed and the longer she looked at him the more her mouth started to water. She clenched her hands to stop from doing anything stupid like reach for him.

'You don't want to make this easy, do you?'

'Not on your life.' And then it seemed as if he almost might smile. 'I have no intention of making it easy for you to walk away from me.'

She had to bend at the waist and draw in a breath, draw in her courage. She straightened. 'I know you don't think the distance between here and Sydney is prohibitive, but I do. I'm not into long distance relationships.'

'But if I set up a practice in either Newcastle or Maitland that problem won't exist. Did you know,' he said pleasantly as if they were talking about nothing more innocuous than the weather, 'that Maitland is one of the fastest growing regional centres in the state at the moment?'

He would relocate. For her?

No!

'Your mother doesn't like me and she's been through enough.'

'Once she gets to know you properly, my mother will love you.'

Her eyes suddenly narrowed. 'Is that why you hassled me so much about going to university? Because in my current "uneducated" state— at least in your and my family's estimation—I wouldn't be good enough for you all otherwise?'

'I'm not even going to dignify that with an answer.' He glared. 'I can see how this stupid inferiority complex of yours has been created by your parents and Phillip.'

'Stupid?' Her mouth worked but no other words emerged.

He stabbed a finger at her. 'I have never wanted anything for you but your happiness. A happiness you're pig-headedly determined to avoid.'

'Pig-headed?' She ground her teeth together. She told herself he had a right to his anger. She was dashing his hopes, hurting him. She tried to settle a mantle of rationality about her. 'We haven't known each other long enough to fall in love.'

He was quiet for a long moment. His eyes never left her face and it was all she could do not to fidget. 'I believe that's true of you,' he finally said, 'but it's not true for me.'

Her stomach gave a sickening lurch.

'It's why I've tried to take things slow.'

She flashed back to her hotel room last Saturday night.

'I fell in love with you the moment you ordered me to take a deep breath and relish the day.'

'Because I reminded you of Danny.' He was in love with a mirage!

'Because you reminded me that the world was good, that life could be good again and that it should be lived.'

The mirage vanished. He loved her? He truly loved her? She tried to gather her scattered thoughts, tried to seize hold of her common sense. 'Do you have an answer for everything?'

'Of course I do. I'm a lawyer.'

A laugh shot out of her, just like that. *This is no time for laughing!* She snapped her mouth shut.

Aidan's face gentled. The afternoon had started to cool, although they weren't far enough into autumn to need sweaters yet. A flock of sulphur-crested cockatoos wheeled around an ancient gum tree further up the hill, their raucous cries filling the air and masking the soft chirrup of a flock of rainbow lorikeets that swooped through the olive grove, heading for the bottlebrush trees on the opposite hill.

She tried to not let it all filter into her soul and relax her—or relax her guard.

'Quinn, what are you really afraid of?'

She moistened her lips. 'That you will eventually accuse me of ruining your life.'

'You'll only ruin it if you walk away.'

His eyes urged her to believe him. Her heart wavered, but she shook her head. They were just words and while she didn't doubt that Aidan meant them in the present moment she had no faith in their longevity.

She prayed for strength. 'You and your family, Aidan, you come from the same world as my parents, the same world as Phillip and his parents. Phillip's parents told him, and me, that I would ruin his life. Before he left, Phillip told me that was true—that I had wrecked his life. Your family believes the exact same thing. And eventually you will too.' She gripped her hands tightly in front of her. 'I'm sorry but I'm not prepared to go through all that again.'

He stared at her. And then his face changed, darkening until thunder practically rolled off his brow and lightning flashed from his eyes. A torrent of angry words shot out of him, most of them not repeatable.

'Of all the idiotic, cock-brained ideas!'

She blinked. Her shoulders started to hunch as he continued with a list of adjectives to describe her way of thinking. Her wrong-headed way of thinking, according to him. Aidan had never yelled at her before. Not really. And it was strange to discover that she hated it. Really, deep down in her gut hated it. She'd finally snapped his control. And she hated that too. Because...

She loved him.

She'd have laughed at the irony, only she didn't have the heart for it. She might love him, but that didn't change a damn thing. She already knew that love wasn't always enough.

He wheeled away from her, only to wheel back

again. 'So, in essence, this all comes down to courage and the fact you have none?'

She stiffened at that. She might've lost her heart, but she still had her pride. 'I beg your pardon?' The way her voice shook, though, destroyed the effect of the iciness she'd tried to inject.

'You demanded courage from me when I was dealing with my mother.'

'That was completely different!'

'How?' he shot back. 'I wasn't leading the life I should've been leading. Just as you're not leading the life you should be leading.'

'Yes I am!' But, while they held vehemence, her words lacked conviction.

'You want to know your problem, Quinn?'

She folded her arms. 'What, I only have the one?' She knew she was being immature but she couldn't help it.

'You don't believe you're worth fighting for.'

Her mouth dried.

His eyes were hard, but strangely gentle too. 'I can slay all the other dragons for you. I can offer you all the assurances in the world. But this particular dragon is one you have to slay for yourself.'

He was going to walk away now, just as she'd

wanted him to. And everything inside her wanted to sob.

His face twisted. 'Damn it, do you really think I'm like your parents? Do you really think I'm like Phillip?'

Her head rocked back. Of course not! But...

But what?

The ground lurched beneath her feet. She tried to steady herself against the branch of an olive tree, but it was thin and threatened to snap. She reeled over to a weathered fence post and leaned against it, careful not to catch herself on the barbed wire. She'd have to ask Mara why they had barbed wire on the property—an idle thought that filtered into her head and out again almost immediately.

She glanced across at Aidan. 'No.' The word croaked out of her. 'I don't think you're like Phillip.'

The hard light in his eyes died, replaced with an uncertainty that tore at her. 'And?'

She moistened her lips. That fact changed everything. If Aidan wasn't like the others—and she knew with everything inside her that he wasn't—then...

'Quinn?'

'It means something about my reasoning is wrong.' She slid down to the ground. 'I'm… I'm trying to work out just what that is.'

He lowered himself to the ground. Reaching out, he took her hand. 'I'm not rushing you, I swear I'm not, but…do you think there's even the slightest chance that you could ever love me?'

Her throat ached. 'Oh, I love you, Aidan, there's no doubt about that.' She held up a hand to keep him where he was when he made as if to gather her up in his arms. Tears burned behind her eyes but she refused to let them fall. 'The thing is, you see, I know that sometimes love isn't enough.'

He stared at her and she swore she saw the life drain out of his face inch by inch. The lump in her throat nearly choked her.

'So that's it, is it?' The words dropped out of him, flat and colourless.

Was it? Slowly she shook her head. 'You're not like Phillip. You're not like my parents. I… I need to think that through more thoroughly.' She had to work out what it meant for them—if it meant anything for them.

He continued to stare at her, but she couldn't tell what he was thinking.

'You said you wouldn't rush me!'

He dragged a hand down his face.

She chafed her arms against the rising tide of fear that threatened to swallow her. 'If you give me an ultimatum—make a decision now or else—I… I would have to tell you goodbye.' It almost killed her to say it, but she forced the words out all the same.

He shook his head as if it were a weight he could barely lift. 'I'm not going to give you an ultimatum, Quinn.'

But his face had gone grey and lines fanned out from his mouth and she had to close her eyes. 'Forgive me for dragging this out, Aidan,' she croaked. 'But I have to be sure.'

She set her back against the post and pushed upright. 'Not just for my sake, but for Robbie and Chase's too. And for yours.'

With that she turned and headed for the house.

'Quinn!'

It was a cry of raw pain. Tears scalded her eyes. 'I'll call you. I promise.' She didn't turn around. She didn't break stride. She kept her eyes fixed forward.

Quinn spent the next week missing Aidan so much her mind refused to answer a single question she needed it to. And those questions went around and around in an endless litany, denying her even a moment of peace. What if Vera never warmed to her or the boys? What if Aidan's friends refused to accept her, convinced she wasn't good enough for him? Would she be able to cope with seeing her parents at other society 'dos'? What if Aidan regretted setting up a practice locally? What if he found himself pining for his firm in Sydney? He'd blame her. What would she do if he broke her heart? It'd send her into the kind of spin she shied from even thinking about.

What if...? What if...? What if...?

She woke in the middle of the night, cheeks wet, and aching for him with everything she had. She stood on the brink of something amazing and exhilarating that could end in disaster. And she couldn't work out if it was worth it or not.

The following Saturday night she and Mara played Monopoly with the boys. Robbie turned to her. 'Mum, do you think I'll ever find a girl I'll want to marry and who'll want to marry me too?'

She handed Chase the dice for his turn. 'I'm sure you will, honey.'

'But Alison at school says I have to marry her!'

Mara chuckled. Quinn sucked her lip into her mouth and bit on it until she could school her features. 'I promise you don't have to marry anyone that you don't want to.'

He gazed at her gloomily. 'But she's nice. I like her. So why don't I want to marry her when she wants to marry me?'

Ah… 'That's the way it goes sometimes, honey. We can be friends with lots and lots of people and we can like them lots and lots, but it doesn't mean we want to marry them. You can't force someone to want to marry you. It doesn't work that way.'

He stared back and finally nodded. 'Okay.'

He seemed happy to take her word for it.

'Is Aidan going to visit us tomorrow?'

She didn't like the way the conversation moved from marriage to Aidan as if…as if it were some logical leap. She fought back a frown. 'I don't think so.'

'Doesn't he like us any more?'

'Sure he does,' Chase chimed in. 'He likes Mum and us best of all. He was sad in Perth. But he wasn't sad when he was with us.'

It took all her strength to choke back a sob. 'Bedtime,' she croaked.

She fell into her chair after putting the boys to bed. Mara pushed a mug of tea across to her. She tried to dredge up a smile. 'Some days they're exhausting.'

Mara merely raised an eyebrow.

Quinn burst into tears.

'Sorry,' she mumbled when she finally had control of them.

Mara sipped her tea. 'Would it be of any interest to you to know that Aidan is staying at the Ross's bed and breakfast at the end of the lane?'

Quinn shot to her feet. He was? Really? She half turned towards the door and then halted. She sat again and chafed her arms.

'Are you afraid of being happy, Quinn?'

She curled her hands around her mug. 'I'm afraid of making another mistake.' And then all those questions that had been plaguing her came pouring out—about his mother and his friends and his job and her parents and what ifs galore.

Mara sat back and surveyed her. 'Does what your parents think have any bearing on your decision to see Aidan again or not?'

'No, of course not.'

Mara didn't say anything, but she lifted that

darn eyebrow again. 'Aidan is a grown man. And an intelligent one. He knows his own mind.'

She hunched over her mug. 'You're saying I should extend the same trust to him that I do to myself.'

Mara remained silent. Quinn stared into her tea. Suddenly, just like that, everything stilled. Her head snapped up. She'd been hiding behind all of those issues when…when it all came down to a simple question of trust.

Did she trust Aidan?

She shot to her feet. 'The B&B at the end of the lane?'

'That's right.'

Quinn grabbed a wrap from the hook by the door and set off down their lane at a run. She didn't even stop to catch her breath when she reached the B&B, but burst up to the front door and knocked.

She stared blankly at the man who answered. Oh! She kicked herself. Of course Aidan wouldn't answer the door. 'Hello, Mr Ross, it's Quinn Laverty from the olive farm. I understand that Aidan Fairhall is staying here and I wondered if I could have a word with him.'

'Sorry, love, but he's not here.'

He'd left? Her shoulders sagged. She backed up a step. 'I'm sorry to have bothered you.' The words almost choked her. 'Goodnight, Mr Ross.'

She turned away. The door closed behind her, shutting her out in the dark. Tears stung her eyes. She tossed her pashmina around her shoulders and held on tight. Of course Aidan had left. What hope had she given him?

'Quinn?'

She halted mid-sniffle. With a heart that barely dared to hope, she turned. 'Aidan? But…but Mr Ross said…'

He'd said that Aidan *wasn't there*. He hadn't said Aidan had decamped back to Sydney.

'I went out for a walk.'

She couldn't drag her gaze from him.

He shifted his weight. 'You wanted to see me?'

A smile built through her. He was here and it had to mean something. It had to mean he hadn't given up on her. Oh, how she loved him! 'Shall I be a hundred per cent honest?'

He folded his arms. 'It's the only way.'

She pulled in a breath, pulled her wrap about her more securely. 'I've spent all week wanting to see you, Aidan.'

'All you had to do was pick up the phone.'

She took a step closer, breathed him in. 'I've not just wanted it, but craved it with everything I am. It freaked me out.'

'I see.'

He stared at her. In the moonlight his face looked beautiful but grim and her heart caught. 'Yes, you probably do. You've seen everything much clearer than I have.'

Something quickened in his face. Suddenly she recognised what it was—hope. 'Oh! I'm not trying to drag this out and make it harder for you, Aidan! I love you. I want to be with you. I want there to be an *us*. If that's what you still—'

She didn't get any further. She found herself in Aidan's arms, caught up in a vortex of desire, relief, frustration and remembered pain as his mouth came down on hers and they kissed like wild things rather than the polite civilised people they pretended to be to the world. When they eventually broke apart they were both breathing heavily. Quinn rested her forehead against his jaw. 'Wow.'

He cupped her face and drew away to stare down at her. 'You mean it?'

'Yes.'

He smiled then and it held so much joy it swept all of the old pain away. 'I love you, Quinn.'

'I love you, Aidan.'

'I love your boys too. I'm going to be the best father I can be to them.'

Father?

He grinned at the way her eyes widened. 'When I ask you to marry me you are going to say yes, aren't you?'

She didn't even hesitate. 'Yes.'

'Excellent. Now that we have the important points out of the way, you want to tell me how you *finally* came to the right conclusion—that we *could* work and that we *should* be together?'

She smiled up at him. 'I only realised it all a moment or two before I came hurtling up the lane to find you. All of those reasons I'd been giving you for why we couldn't be together, I realised they were just issues I'd been hiding behind. The question I should've been asking myself was— Do I trust you? When I finally asked the right question, it all fell into place.'

She sobered. 'I do trust you, Aidan. I asked myself what you'd do if you were unhappy in a relationship.' She shook her head. 'You wouldn't just walk away. You wouldn't seethe or fester in silence either. You'd work at making things better.' Communication was important to him. 'You don't have a shallow heart. You have a heart that is deep and true and will weather storms.'

His eyes darkened. 'I'll weather any storm with you, Quinn. But do you believe that you have a heart that is deep and true too?'

That was the risk Aidan took, she suddenly saw.

Her heart pounded. Ice touched her nape, but she refused to let the fear overcome her. She thought back over her life and how she'd dealt with her parents…with Phillip…and with her two gorgeous boys. Gradually a weight started to lift and the chill receded. 'Yes,' she breathed, beaming her love straight at him. 'Yes, I do.'

His hands went around her waist, drawing her closer. 'My lovely girl,' he whispered against her lips.

She cupped his face in her hands. 'I'm sorry it took me so long to realise the truth. Tell me you forgive me. I love you, Aidan. I love you with my whole heart.'

'Sweetheart—' he grinned down at her '—there's nothing to forgive. I needed you to be as sure about us as I was.'

She sobered. 'And are you?'

'I love you. I want to build a life with you. I have never been surer of anything in my life.'

His lips descended to hers and if she'd had any lingering doubts they'd have melted away. She flung her arms around his neck and kissed him back with all the love in her overflowing heart.

* * * * *

LET'S TALK
Romance

For exclusive extracts, competitions and special offers, find us online:

📘 facebook.com/millsandboon

📷 @millsandboonuk

🐦 @millsandboon

Or get in touch on 0844 844 1351*

For all the latest titles coming soon, visit millsandboon.co.uk/nextmonth

Want even more
ROMANCE?

Join our bookclub today!